DRUDGE MATCH

MATTHEW A. GOODWIN

Independently published

Copyright© 2022 Matthew A. Goodwin

ISBN Number 978-1-7340692-6-6

Edited by Joanne Paulson

Cover design by Christian Bentulan

Check out the end of the book for a glossary of terms.

If you are reading this,
This book is for you.
I could never have
Written these without your support.
Thank you.

PROLOGUE

It was as if billions of pixels were fading at once as Moss left the program in his mind. He was back in the real world. He had no idea how long he had been unconscious, but when he blinked back to reality, he knew it hadn't been more than a few minutes.

He saw Derek Sterling, the head of D2E, the world's largest entertainment conglomerate and secret ally, looking down at him. The man was tired and wounded after everything they had been through but his eyes were clear.

"You all right?"

"No," Moss said as he remembered what had just happened. Ever since Gibbs and Ynna's wedding night, the digital construct of his father's personality, which had been imbued into a program and uploaded to Moss's neural chip, had been trying to get his attention. Moss had been able to hold it at bay for a long time with a combination of sheer will and dampener pills, but the program had finally broken through.

He had never seen his father look the way he had-neither in real life nor in the program. It had upset him deeply and forced him to question everything he had ever done.

"We have to go!" Derek shouted as he gestured toward the bank of screens projected along one wall. They were in the studio's main control room and the agents who had been attacking them were on the move again. Reaching down a hand, he helped Moss to his feet.

"I thought we dealt with all these guys," Moss said, twirling his machine gun towards the door. Seeing this, Rude Von 'Tude, the D2E shock jock turned double agent, looked terrified and hustled over to them.

"You have to keep me safe, too," he pleaded and Moss swallowed hard. Keeping two unarmed civilians safe amid the heat of battle was going to be difficult, but Moss moved them into positions behind some of the consoles. He took cover too, being careful to keep his weapon trained at the door.

From the periphery, he watched as the agents made their way toward the room. There were a lot of them. Moss couldn't even count how many and they were all streaming in his direction. Earlier, he had had a plan and traps that would meet them along the way; but this time it was just him and a machine gun. Glancing down at the digital display on the side of the weapon, he also saw how few rounds he had left. He sighed and flipped it to semiautomatic.

They were getting close to the door, close enough that he could hear their footsteps in real time. Rude sounded like he was muttering something in a language Moss didn't recognize and Derek was trying to calm himself with slow breaths. In all likelihood, both of these men would be dead soon. With the onslaught facing them, he probably would be too. But before the agents reached the door, they all turned back.

The images on the screens erupted in muzzle flash and commotion.

In his mind, through his neural communication, he heard Gibbs say, *The eagles are coming*!

"Stay here!" he commanded the two men as he rushed towards the door. He threw it open to see the backs of the armored agents and beyond them his friends on the attack. They had ambushed the agents at the end of the hallway but the agents had pushed their way back into a waiting area. There, Ynna was hacking away at one with a nanoblade, Gibbs was taking shots at them from behind the couch and Moss's fiancé, Issy, was firing bursts from behind the vending machine.

Moss moved stealthily down the corridor, toward the line of backs, and ducked just inside the door to an office to provide himself some cover. He popped his head out and aimed his weapon, letting out a small exhale before taking some shots. Despite his aim, most of the shots dinged uselessly off the agent's armor; but one bullet managed to find its way between the gaps. The agent screamed and turned, firing bursts back at him and shredding the thin wall that he was using as protection. He dropped to the ground, but the distraction was enough to allow Moss's friends to push forward. One by one the agents were killed, and soon Moss was able to pop back out, using his last three bullets to take down the last agent.

As he emerged from the office, Issy ran to him and wrapped him in a tight embrace.

Kissing him on the cheek, she said, "We did it!"

Moss smiled. "People have seen it? The message is out there?"

Issy pulled back and beamed at him, her big chestnut eyes full of tears and hope. "They saw it. The world saw it. And people are ready to fight back."

She studied his face. "Is everything okay?"

"No," Moss admitted, "but I'll tell you later."

She looked at him sternly. "You'd better."

"I will," Moss said and meant it. He had to tell her what happened, what he had done and what the program had done.

"But now," he said as Gibbs and Ynna hustled over, "we have two other people who need our help."

He guided them down the hallway towards the control room, and announced as he walked in, "Derek, Rude, we have to get here before they send more agents after us." His eyes went wide. "What the fuck?"

Moss's heart broke as he saw Derek slumped against the wall, his hands pressing the spot on his belly where he had clearly been shot with his own weapon. Rude was standing over him, his graying, curly black hair waving wildly as he turned the pistol on Moss and his friends.

"I had to do it!" Rude shrieked. "They were going to kill them. They were going to kill my parents! This is what I had to do. Or part of it … anyway …" He appeared to be in shock. "Maybe they let them live because I did this."

Moss grimaced. "We could've gotten them out for you," he said. "I told you that you didn't have to do anything like this anymore."

"You don't know what it's like!" Rude yelled, waving the weapon wildly in their direction.

"It doesn't matter what it's like!" Moss yelled back, raising his own weapon. "The man who's dying on the floor is one of the keys to our victory and you fucking shot him."

"I had to! You must understand that!"

As Moss was about to pull the trigger of his rifle, Rude's head burst open in a shower of blood and his body crumpled to the ground. Moss wheeled around to see Ynna raising her hands in mock defensiveness.

"Ooh, no, I killed a disgusting bigot … sue me."

Moss shook his head. "It's not that," he said. "It's that *I* was gonna kill him."

"You snooze, you lose. Real leaders move quickly," she said, and slapped Moss patronizingly on the ass.

Derek let out a groan and Moss rushed over to him, putting his hand on his stomach to help stem the flow of blood. "You'll be all right, we'll get you help."

"In movies," Derek said through ragged breaths. "I always thought it was ridiculous when a character could tell they were going to die, but you can. The second I took the shot, I knew. I can feel myself bleeding out. Feel myself ... fading."

"No, no, no," Moss said. "We'll get you help."

"You *can* help me with something," Derek said and his voice had the tone of somebody who was, in fact, dying. Derek pulled the hand holding his palmscreen away from his gut. "Can you get the blood off this?"

Moss tried using the sleeve of his suit jacket to clean the blood off the man's screen, but the mesh was so much like skin that the blood simply seeped in more quickly. Issy came over, already unscrewing the cap to a canteen. She poured water over the screen and Moss wiped it once again with his sleeve. The blood was in the cracks and crevices, already drying, but enough of it came off to make the screen operable.

Derek's hand trembled as he curled his fingers around to tap the screen built into his palm. Moss's friends gathered around as Derek finished what he was doing and looked up.

"Just transferred all my funds to The Conservation and ownership of D2E to you guys. You can do it now," he said and a broad smile crossed his face. "You can take the world back from the wealthy one percent and give it to the people who have had their lives kept from them for too long."

Moss took the man's hands in his and looked into his fading eyes. "Thank you," he said. "For everything you've done. You are the reason we are here and you are the reason we will be able to defeat the megas. Thank you," he repeated.

"I was so happy to be a part of this," Derek said and Moss wondered what kind of bravery it had taken for this man to do this. He had lived his whole life in the viper's nest and had to funnel money through clandestine means, knowing that if he was ever caught, the other members of the Amalgamated Interests Council would find a way to have him killed. It was a remarkable thing.

His head rolled back, his dirty brown hair now slick with blood and his bloodshot eyes glassy. Moss put his other hand under Derek's back and lifted him. He had to make eye contact with him one more time.

"I promise you your sacrifice won't be in vain. We will help all those other little kids growing up like you did."

Derek smiled, but his eyes were in some far-off place. "Thank you. No more kids like me."

"No more kids like you," he promised and felt all the remaining power in the man's body fade. In an instant, he went from a person to a body. The hands fell and no more muscle supported him.

Moss felt a tear burn his cheek. He had met this man only about an hour earlier and had thought him his enemy at the time, but now he felt the gravity of the loss. Derek had funded their fight thanklessly for years and died for it.

He had given his life for this cause and died without fanfare or recognition, just as so many others had done. Moss hated it, hated the price people were having to pay. ThutoCo had still managed to kill him. These agents, who were little more than a way for the company to keep Moss off their scent, had managed to complete their mission.

He stood and turned; his teeth gritted so hard that his jaw felt like it was going to pop off his face. Issy stepped over and put her hand on his chest.

"I'm so sorry, Moss."

"He was a hero," Moss said. "Another silent hero I would never have even heard about . We have to honor him, honor his sacrifice. We will destroy ThutoCo once and for all and rid this planet of the fucking companies who have oppressed it for too long- all of them.

"Too many people have died. Too much pain has been caused. It's time to end this, time to turn this planet around before it's too late. We will save the people *and* we will save the planet. With the money he just gave The Conservation, there is an actual hope that we can do both."

All his friends were smiling at him, looking inspired and ready to take action.

"Now," he said with a proud finality, "let's go obliterate ThutoCo for good."

PART I

CHAPTER 1

Moss carried the bundle of wood to the ditch and dropped it in.

"Says here that we could also use some dry leaves to get it started," Issy said, looking up from the paper she had brought.

Despite his rousing speech, they needed time to actually form a plan to dismantle ThutoCo and he had promised himself that he would spend some time with Issy. So, here he was. Looking up at the trees, he smiled as he took in a deep breath. They were out in the wilderness without masks or ventilators or breathing apparatus or filters. The air was so natural that it almost hurt the nose so unaccustomed to anything but the synthetic.

Even though they had gone public with the fact that the areas around the city weren't actually poisonous, the people were still scared and almost none had left the city. This meant that anything that had not been converted into fields of profit root or solar panels by ThutoCo was still untouched country.

"You can probably just use that pamphlet, there, as kindling," Moss said with a chuckle as he knelt and plucked up some dry leaves.

Issy rolled her eyes. "Right, but then I wouldn't have it anymore," she said and folded the paper to tuck it into her shorts pocket. They were both dressed in simple T-shirts and short pants with hiking boots. Gibbs had not stopped laughing for a solid ten minutes when he saw them.

Issy walked over to the edge of a cliff and looked out over the pristine wilderness. It stretched on for as far as the eye could see — nothing but trees and rocks and hills. The colors were spectacular. In the fading light, the world glowed.

"I still can't believe it."

"Me neither," Moss said after leaving a little pile of leaves next to the sticks and joining her at the vista. "We were told this one thing for so long and didn't have any reason not to believe it. Even being here now, it still feels …"

"Wrong?"

"Yeah." Moss nodded. "Exactly."

"To think that they kept us from this, kept everyone from this, just so they could use the rest of the space for themselves … I still can't believe it," she repeated.

Moss put his arm around her. "I suppose the one benefit is that we have it to ourselves right now."

Issy turned and looked up at him, the orange light of the setting sun glowing in her eyes. "That's something, anyway." She nuzzled into him and from this spot above the valley, they watched in silence as the sun disappeared over the horizon.

Just before the dark engulfed them, they heard a branch crack before a massive shape flew over them. The owl's wings beat silently as it left its daytime perch and glided down and out of sight to hunt. Moss felt his mouth fall open as he gazed in wonder.

Issy smiled at him and put her hand on his chest. "What is it? I know I've asked you before, but what is it about the animals?"

Moss shook his head. "I think about it all the time, especially when I get made fun of for it. I guess it's just that every time I see an animal, it feels like it fits. Each one has a role and they play it perfectly, bringing balance to a perfect planet.

"We are the opposite. People spread, take and destroy everything. We took so much from this planet that we had to leave and explore the galaxy for more supplies. And when taking over the planet wasn't enough, we also took over each other. There is no natural balance with humans; it's a devastating hierarchy.

"I think I had to understand that to help make this fight mine. For so long I was just going along with it, being led by the nose by this person or that. By Burn or my family. By trying to honor or avenge people like Stan and Rosetta. The fight wasn't mine for too long, but now I have my own reasons to fight. I want to help bring equality to the humans but also to help places like this flourish.

"I love that we're alone here, but I want others to be able to see and experience this. We grew up in a plastic world with digital escapism. And that's all we would ever have known if not for those few who sought to free us. Now, I seek to free those who are like us."

"That's a perfect answer," Issy said with a smile. "Perfect answer to a question I didn't ask, but a perfect answer."

Moss chuckled. "I don't know … they're just cool."

"I mean, I guess," Issy shrugged. "I think they're neat but I don't think I'll ever quite get it."

"And why do you want to do this?" Moss asked. "I know you didn't just come here for me."

"I told you; I want to change the world," Issy said so sincerely that Moss had no doubt. "But I just hate seeing wrong. And there's so much wrong. I joined BurbSec because, even on a small scale, I wanted to help right wrongs and make people feel safe. This is just that on a much larger scale."

Moss fished the lighter from his pocket and walked over to their small campfire ditch. He had never camped before, and while he was excited about being in nature, it was also a bit overwhelming. He lit one of the leaves and dropped it under the sticks, and soon the fire was crackling to life. The sun set slowly but it stayed warm as the two sat on a log beside the fire.

They ate the meals that they had brought with them and enjoyed the sound of the fire in the wilderness around them. But even with that, it was quiet, a true quiet; and when they looked into the distance, it was a true dark.

Moving on to a bedroll, they stared up at the stars. Moss had seen one or two before but the light from the city had made it nearly impossible. For the first time, gazing up at all the little white dots, he appreciated how small they were. The off-world colonies had always been little more than a concept to him, but looking up at the vast space now, it seemed only fitting that there was life all around them.

Issy leaned over and kissed Moss on the cheek, nuzzling him from her position beside him, her head tucked up over his shoulder. He smiled. They had done so much, and though there had been an immensely high price, they were close to finishing it. They had kicked the Carcer Corporation out of the city and installed their own person at its head. They had taken over the airwaves and the Internet and they had crippled ThutoCo's ability to fight by taking out the headquarters of its Zeta military force.

Thinking about all this, and how close they were to finally ridding the planet of the megas, Moss's heart was full. He leaned over and kissed Issy, taking her hand in his and tilting it to see the ring he had given her. His mother's ring. Looking at it, she smiled and said, "Yes, by the way."

"What?" Moss asked.

Issy chuckled. "When you proposed, I gave you a whole big speech, but I never actually said yes. So, yes."

"Oh, good." Moss laughed. A warm breeze danced through the campsite and he kissed Issy again, realizing that he was happy for the first time in a very long time. "I love you, Is."

"I love you, too, Moss," Issy said and nuzzled close.

They lay in silence for a long time, gazing up at the stars, before Issy finally said, "So, I have to ask ... what happened at D2E?"

His moment of reverie ended and he felt he might throw up. He remembered his father's face as he screamed, "How could you? My mother! Your grandmother! How could you?"

The digital recreation of the man who lived in Moss's mind punched his son. It beat and hit him and Moss deserved it. As the first blows landed, Moss didn't know if it was the program or his own unconscious controlling the program; but he felt he deserved it either way.

The program told his brain that he tasted blood as he licked his lips and his father pushed him away, staring at him in anguish and heartbreak.

"I had to," Moss said.

"No," his father told him flatly. "You didn't. There's always another way. If I taught you anything it's that there's always another way."

Overwhelmed by anguish and sadness, Moss squeaked, "There isn't always another way and it was grandma who taught me that."

Moss's father collapsed onto the couch, burying his face in his hands and sobbing. Moss didn't know if he was weeping for his loss over what his son had become or maybe something more. He walked over to him and sat beside him on the couch, the cushions giving and forcing their shoulders together.

"Dad," he said, choking on his own tears. "I know you're not proud of who I've become but doing what I had to do made me the person that I need to be to see this through. It's not just about your technology anymore. It's about so much more. And ..." Moss struggled to find the words. "To see it done, I can't do it the other way. Real change requires hard people making hard decisions."

Moss's father looked up at him with miserable crimson eyes. "You may be right, but I never wanted you to become a hard person. I wanted you to be a better person. I wanted you to be the best of me, the best of your mother, and the best of your grandmother."

"I think I am," Moss told him. "I've had to do so much but I've always risen to the occasion. Even when I thought I wouldn't be able to, I did."

"But the things you're doing, the things you've done, it's taken so much from you. I don't want you to give up your soul to save the world."

Moss chuckled and wiped a tear from his cheek. "It's a small price to pay. My soul for the world's soul; I would do it in a heartbeat."

"Admirable as that is," his father said, "it's not what any parent wants to hear. I'm the exact opposite. I would sacrifice this entire world for you."

Moss smiled and put his arm over his father's shoulder. "I know, Dad, but in real life you die for what you believe in. I didn't have you for most of my life because you chose to do what was right for the world. I may have this version of you, but the real man never got to watch me grow up and become this version of myself. You can talk all about your philosophies, but this you was frozen in time when you made the copy.

"Neither of us know what you thought in those last moments — who you wanted me to become or how you felt about the sacrifice you had made. You and Mom both paid the ultimate price to help others and, if what I'm doing now makes me someone you're not proud of, it's just another price I have to pay."

His father shook his head. "I'll never be any less proud of you and it's not even what you did that scares me so much. It's that you thought to do it. It's that you thought it was necessary or that it was justified."

"You weren't there and you will never really understand," Moss said. "She was your mother and I understand that, but she had also become something else. She was hurting people and hurting our cause. She became an agent of vengeance and would have sacrificed anything to hurt those that had hurt her. I made a choice in the moment and I will have to live with it for the rest of my life. But I also saved this cause. She would have dismantled our entire revolution before we saw this thing through to completion. I had to become like her to stop what she had become."

"You're right," he said, "but you're also wrong. I didn't have to be there to know that there was a better way. But also …" he trailed off. "You're right that I'm a personality frozen in time. I don't know what I thought in those last moments. I don't know what the man who was murdered and stolen from his son by ThutoCo would have thought about what you're doing. Honestly, I don't know if the real man would've done the same exact thing you did. I know what this iteration of me thinks, but this has never been the real me."

"That's a hard pill to swallow," Moss said. "I fought so hard to keep this program, to keep you, but maybe it's time I move on. All my friends think it's time to get rid of it, that it's hurting me too much, and maybe they're right."

"If they're saying it, they probably are right. Know that I have no self-preservation instincts programmed into me, but I don't think you should delete it just yet. We've discovered so many secrets about the power your mother imbued into this program. I wouldn't delete it until you've destroyed ThutoCo for good."

Moss grinned and pointed excitedly. "That's what I've been saying!"

"Well, you *are* my son."

He tried to force the memory of that moment from his mind as he turned to look Issy in the eye. The flickering firelight played on her face as he said the words he swore never to speak aloud.

"I killed Sandra."

Issy's face scrunched up in sadness but not it was not a look of surprise. "I know."

CHAPTER 2

"You know?" Moss exclaimed. He had just revealed what he had taken to be an earth-shattering truth and her response was not at all what he expected.

"Moss, my love, I've known you a long time," Issy said quietly. "I watched as your grandmother made you question yourself, doubt yourself. I watched as she drove a wedge between all of us and threatened to separate you from your best friends. I watched her murder a young man whose only crime was helping us. I knew what she had become too. We all did."

"Do the others know?" Moss couldn't help but ask. His head was spinning.

"No," she said with a little smile. "No one knows you like I do. Ynna would never suspect it of you and I don't think Gibbs could even conceptualize something like that."

"It happened so fast," he admitted quietly. "I didn't even have time to think. I hadn't planned it, but in the moment, I knew it had to be done. In a weird way, she was the one who taught me it had to be done. It wasn't just that she was giving me her permission, it was almost as if she was inviting me to do it. She kept testing me and testing me and testing me and then … there was this final test."

"Sounds like her," she said and Moss knew she meant it. She wasn't shining him on or telling him what he needed to hear. She'd never done that and certainly wouldn't with this. If she was saying these things, she meant it. "I'll never forget the look on your face when she shot Zip Thud."

"A lot changed in that moment."

"That's just it. It was written all over your face. It was the look of… betrayal."

Moss nodded slowly as Issy rubbed his back. "Exactly. With her, it had become a series of betrayals. I was so scared of what she was becoming, what she had done and what she was willing to do, that I had to do something I would never have imagined. I killed my own blood relative."

"That's the other thing that I know about you that the others don't," Issy said. "I know that family is different for you. You spent your entire adult life making family out of the people around you: me, my dad, Gibbs and now these guys. *We* were your family. You are related to Sandra, sure; but we were your true family. I know that, the others know it, and your grandmother knew it."

"I told her so," Moss said, remembering her last moment before he put his hand on her back.

The tears came then like a torrent. The pain he'd been holding for so long, the guilt and self-loathing all came pouring out of him. He had done what he had had to do but that understanding hadn't made it any easier. He had thought that doing wrong for the right reasons might make it not hurt so much, but he still felt the weight of what he done every waking second.

It was why his father had been banging at the door of his mind. It was why Moss had beaten the shit out of some stranger behind the bar. There was so much pent up inside him and it was all being released now. Issy wrapped her arms around him and rubbed his back as he released it all. Her touch helped-taking some of his pain and leaving her love.

"You hold onto so much," Issy said. "But we're here for you. I'm here for you. You are not in this alone. You have your family."

Hearing the word brought even more tears. His mother was dead. His father was a digital construct trapped in his mind. And his grandmother had died at his hands. The word family meant something completely different to him now. He wrapped his arms around Issy and held her close. *She* was his family. She was the person he had relied on his whole life and the person who had given him strength. She was the person that would get him through to the end.

"Thank you," Moss said. "For my whole life. For everything. For loving me. For forgiving me. For tolerating me. And for giving me the strength to do what I thought was impossible."

"You've always underestimated yourself," Issy said. "But you have this thing in you, this spark. I always kinda envied it."

Moss laughed. "I could never have imagined you envying me for anything. You were always the toughest of the three of us and the smartest."

"I know, right?" Issy mocked with a wink. "But it wasn't toughness or smarts that I was jealous of. It was that instinct, that killer instinct. Somehow, you could make a split-second decision and it would be the right one. Every time. When I met Sandra, I saw where came from. It's a gift, and even more than me, it'll be the thing that carries you through to the end."

"It's strange to think how close we are to the end, or what feels like the end, anyway," Moss observed.

"There'll be work after," Issy assured him, "but it will be the end. If a handful of former employees manage to bring ThutoCo to its knees, we have to call that the end. You and I can ride off into the sunset."

"What do you want that sunset to be?" he asked, drying his face. "Where do you want to go? What do you want to do?"

She stared at the stars for a long time and then laughed. "Shit, guess I should've given that some thought. I don't really know. I know I want to spend my life with you, but other than that I hadn't really given it much thought. Have you?"

"I have."

After a long while, Issy snorted and asked, "And?"

"I've always known that you want to do good and I think you're going to want to continue to do so even after this. The mayor is putting together an advisory board and I think you should sit on it. I think it would do the world a lot of good to have you designing the rules that help keep people safe."

Issy looked at him in astonishment and a little smile crossed her face. "Without meaning to, I think you just paid me the biggest compliment anybody ever has."

Moss smirked. "It wasn't entirely accidental."

"Even so, that's one of the kindest things anybody's ever said about me, and if Mayor LeBeau will have me, I would love to help establish the future. And you?"

He opened his mouth to start to answer but the way Issy was looking at him, he wondered if she already knew. "What?"

"Oh, we both know that you're going to want to help The Conservation heal the natural world. It's literally the only thing that makes sense for you."

"You got me dead to rights," Moss said. "It's exactly what I want to do."

"That's why you brought us here instead of going to some sweet-ass resort, huh?"

Being caught, Moss felt his face flush. "Maybe…"

"See," Issy said sweetly, "I do know you better than anybody."

She climbed on top of him, put her hands on both sides of his head and looked into his eyes for a long moment before moving closer. When their lips touched, Moss felt the same electric excitement that he had the first time he kissed her. He still got butterflies in his stomach as she began to unbutton her top and his hands still went numb with nervous excitement as she slid off his pants.

He was as in love with her now as he had ever been and he knew that would never fade. The warm air caressed his body as he shifted and slid inside her. The flickering firelight danced over her skin as she moved against him. She ran her hands over his flat stomach and nibbled at his neck.

They moved as one. It was natural and easy. It was pleasure perfected and it was another way Moss knew they were perfect together. Not that he was thinking about it then. All he was thinking about was Issy.

Moss was startled awake by the feeling of basted air rushing over him and the tent that they never made it to having its stakes ripped from the ground as the dropship landed nearby. Moss and Issy were on their feet in an instant, both trying to find something to cover themselves with.

The massive ship set down and the campsite calmed as the two ran to collect their clothes. As they pulled on pants, Ynna jumped from the ship's side door.

"Nice," she said as she saw them. "Woulda been disappointed if this wasn't what you guys were getting into, but I have to say I half expected you to talk all night or some shit."

"What the fuck are you doing here?" Moss shrieked over the sound of the dropship engine.

Ynna's face grew dark. "Get packed up. I'll tell you in the ship."

"Who's flying that thing?" Issy asked as she pulled her shirt on.

Ynna looked back over her shoulder. "Hacked a drudge. No one else knows how to fly it. not since Anders... well, anyhoo, no one else knows how to fly it..."

"This better be serious," Moss said through gritted teeth as he gathered up his stuff.

"You really think I would come to get you if it was anything less than dire?" Ynna scoffed. "I mean, who would want to interrupt all this super-hot bub sex?"

Issy took her palm and pushed it lightly against Ynna's face as she walked towards the ship. "Pain in the ass," she said as she boarded.

"Just leave it," Ynna called as Moss tried to break down the tent. "I'll send the drudge back for it. Let's just get out of here."

Moss nodded and headed for the ship, throwing in his bag before strapping himself beside Issy. Ynna climbed in too, and they were off immediately.

"So, what's up?" Issy asked nervously.

Ynna looked at them from where she was sitting across the ship. "ThutoCo didn't wait around. They started to poison the water supplies, using that shit they used on you in the burbs, but worse. Much worse. It's... it's like the beginning of the second Grade Pandemic."

"Wait…" Moss murmured. "The spores? They're using the spores?"

Ynna nodded gravely. "We are still waiting on word from the burbs, but it's suspected that anyone who lives there is already dead."

"Oh no," Issy said, her face contorting in grief. "Everyone we've ever known," she said, looking at Moss.

It was hard to imagine. He knew ThutoCo was evil but he couldn't believe it would do something like this, would kill all their employees. He thought about all those hexes in all those burbs. He remembered that first flight out, looking back and being amazed at how many of the structures there were. The idea of them all, littered with the dead, was almost too much to bear.

Arthur Smith must have gone mad. When all the news came out about him and what they had done, he must have decided to just be done with everyone.

"In the city?" Moss asked. "You said they're poisoning people in the city too?"

"Seems that way," Ynna said. "We are already using D2E's network to tell everybody to stop drinking water for as long as they can, but people need water to live. And not everybody listens to the news.

"There are some people who are drinking water in defiance of being told what to do and it is already a viral challenge to drink the water. But those are few and far between and," she shrugged with a dark expression, "they'll seal their own fate."

"If this thing spreads…" Moss said, trying to find the words. "The whole city is doomed."

"Pretty much," Ynna agreed.

"What do they want?" Moss asked. "Has ThutoCo made any demands of us or of the mayor's office?"

"That's just it," Ynna said. "They haven't reached out at all or made any demands. ThutoCo hasn't even taken credit, but we've ruled out any other candidates and Seti believes she tracked down the chain of events, tracing it back to ThutoCo."

"But why?" Issy said, her words desperate. "Why do something like this? What's in it for them?"

Moss felt the truth as though he was being hit over the head with it. "They're done with us. ThutoCo and the AIC, they're done with people."

"What?" Ynna and Issy said in unison.

"They don't need us anymore," Moss said. "They'll replace us all with drudges. They will use my father's technology to make the best version of robots in human history. Earth will become entirely populated by drudges with perfect physical forms combined with the creative problem-solving of a human mind fused with a deep learning AI.

"We have become such a nuisance to them that they will just rid the planet of all humans except themselves and turn the entire thing into the largest factory in the galaxy. They will produce food and spices and energy and ship them all off-world. They will become richer than ever before and they won't have us to contend with."

Issy and Ynna just stared at Moss for a long time. "No," Issy said. "These people may be evil, but they're not global genocide evil."

"They are," Ynna said. "I think that's exactly how evil they are."

"No, you guys, no," Issy said but her words betrayed her. She seemed to know it was true even though she couldn't allow herself to believe it.

"It's true, Is," Moss said. "I feel like I know Arthur Smith's mind. He invaded mine once, and now, since being back in the program, I feel the imprint he left. This is what he wants."

"Why?" Issy asked in a whisper.

"I don't know," Moss admitted.

"Who gives a fuck why?" Ynna snapped. "It doesn't matter why they're doing this evil shit, just how are we going to stop them."

"Do you guys have any plans?" Moss asked.

"We only just learned and we're scrambling," Ynna told them. "You have any ideas?"

Moss nodded. "I do. I know exactly where we should go."

.

PART II

CHAPTER 3

They jumped out of the ship even before it landed and ran toward the door to the house. This part of the city was wealthy enough that everybody had their own house, but not so wealthy that the houses weren't touching. The ship had touched down in the street to block traffic, as the three made their way to the door. Moss knocked quickly several times using the same pattern he had used so long ago on the office door. It swung open immediately.

"Moss?" Mr. Greene said in utter astonishment. His former boss at ThutoCo wrapped him in a big hug before stepping back and saying, "I suppose you're here on business."

Moss nodded and Mr. Greene waved them in.

The house was clean and lovely, furnished in glass and white, but there were scuff marks on the wall, handprints on the windows and toys tucked under the couches. Mr. Greene greeted Issy and Ynna and closed the door behind them before calling out, "Brian, Millicent, come in here, please, and say hi to my friends."

A moment later, Mr. Greene's husband and their child walked into the room. Unlike Mr. Greene, Brian looked tired and scared. Like the rest of them, he had escaped from under ThutoCo's thumb and now lived in constant fear that they would come for him. Despite his obvious worry, he was well put together, wearing fine slacks and a tucked button-down shirt, the sleeves rolled to three quarters. His hair was beginning to gray and his glasses were showing signs of age with one pin sticking up slightly to indicate a home repair. He had the look of someone trying his best to hide his emotions and not entirely succeeding.

Millicent, on the other hand, strode into the room like she owned the place. Because, Moss realized, she did. That made Moss happy. When his parents died and he began working for Mr. Greene, Moss had always thought of the man as both mentor and father figure and it was nice to see him as an actual father – but also nice to see him humbled a bit.

Her blonde hair was thin and though it appeared to have been well cut, it was disheveled and didn't appear to have been washed as recently as Mr. Greene would have probably liked. Her hands and arms were stained with remnants of some earlier art project and her eyes were big and bright. She wore rainbow-striped pants under a D2E princess dress under a fireman's jacket.

She moved to wrap her arms around Mr. Greene's legs, poking her head out from behind. It was not an act of fear of the new faces, but a simple desire to be close to her father.

"Millie, these are my friends Ynna and Issy and, I'm sorry I can't quite remember your name…"

Ynna and Issy snickered and Moss rolled his eyes. "Oof, dad jokes right out of the gate."

"Oh, please," Brian said with a chuckle, "Tom trafficked in 'dad jokes' long before he was a father."

Moss had to give him that and smiled as the man shook hands all around. Moss knelt and smiled at Millicent. "Making sure to give your dads a hard time?" Moss joked and the girl looked at him with mild confusion. She looked to be about four or five; Moss couldn't remember how old she had been when the men had adopted her.

"I'm Moss," he said, holding out a hand which she shook firmly with her tiny hand.

"Hi," she said, and after a beat informed him, "My friend Bodhi and I play ninjas, and even though he has more ninja weapons I always win."

Moss smiled. "Well, that's neat."

"Yeah," the little girl agreed triumphantly.

"Hey, Mil," Brian said. "Can you run to your room and grab that holo drum set to show these guys?"

"Oh, yeah, good idea, Dad," Millicent said and gave a big thumbs-up before running from the room.

Mr. Greene cocked his head at his husband. "I thought we donated that."

"We did," Brian said with a little smile.

"Then let's get down to business," Mr. Greene said, turning back to his guests and gesturing for them to sit on the couches. "You're here about the water supply?"

"Yes," Moss said.

"I'm afraid I can't help you. I've been racking my brain trying to think of anyone at ThutoCo who might have some information about what's going on or how to fix it, but I can't think of anyone. I'm sorry if you feel like you wasted a trip."

"I like that you seem to believe you're the only one who has any possible connections," Brian said in the tone of scolding partners everywhere. "You didn't even think to ask me?"

"I didn't mean any offense," Mr. Greene defended himself, and once again Moss felt a little weird. Even though he had known Mr. Greene personally for quite some time, he still thought of him as his boss and it was strange to see him in this different light.

"Ignorance of the law was not an excuse," Brian said, folding his arms.

"Hey, guys, I hate to be a dick, but can you save the shit for when people aren't dying from drinking water?" Ynna said.

Brian turned to her and seemed to remember the stakes. "Sorry. I just don't like feeling as if I can't contribute."

"We all want you to contribute, Bri," Mr. Greene put in.

"You could have made that clear from the start," Brian said under his breath but then turned to the others.

"A few years ago, an email went out from the research department to all senior managers. Tom, being a middle manager, didn't receive it. The message discussed research being done by a woman who believed she could cure the spore infections and eliminate the need for the misting towers around the city.

"As you expect, the email was unsent and deleted by IT, even though some had already seen it. And that scientist, she also disappeared. We all knew better than to ask questions, and frankly I assumed she had been disappeared six feet into the earth, if you take my meaning."

"We do," Moss said, wishing that Brian would cut to the chase.

"She was not, as it turns out. She was sent to the city with that pittance that the company provides when it wants a person to be swallowed entirely by the mean streets. Turns out they don't have to outright kill someone to ensure they don't survive," Brian explained, seeming to take pride in the clever way he was unfolding the story. He gestured wildly with his hands and seemed very pleased that he was the center of attention.

"Do you know where she is?" Ynna snapped and Moss was relieved that she butted in.

"Yes," Brian said. "A few months ago, I ran into her at the grocery store and we got to talking. I didn't know who she was at first — we just recognized each other as ThutoCo survivors — but eventually I put two and two together. She has a son who's about the same age as Millie or maybe a year younger… though it could just be that her son was born big and Millie is a pipsqueak. Either way, they are close enough in age that they would be able to play together –"

"Love," Mr. Greene interjected. "Just tell them how to contact her."

"Right, yes, of course," Brian said as if he didn't realize that he had been vamping a bit. "I have her number right here." He opened his hand and began scrolling through the screen in his palm.

"Would you mind giving her a call?" Moss asked.

But even as the words left his mouth, Brian was already doing it. The whole screen showed on his palm as they waited anxiously, but there was no answer. Without having to be asked, Brian called a second time. When there was no answer again, he looked up at them and said, "Given everything that's going on, she might not answer the phone for someone calling about a play date."

Moss heard a neural communication and they all stood as Ynna said, "I have Seti running down their address and we'll head over there now just to be sure."

"You want me to go with you? I'm the one she knows," Brian offered and they shook their heads.

"No, thank you," Moss said "You stay here and safe. Millie needs you a lot more than we do, and I expect things are gonna get worse before they get any better."

Brian put on a brave face and nodded, but Moss could tell he was a little disappointed. "This lead may help us save the city. Seriously, thank you, Brian."

That was what the man needed to hear and he smiled before puffing himself up a bit. Moss was happy that he could give Brian this little victory, this little moment. He was scared and overwhelmed, and those emotions leaking from him wouldn't be helpful as the days continued to get darker. Hopefully helping the good guys succeed against impossible odds would help him feel better.

As they got up to leave, Moss heard Brian offer, "Do they need all of her information, everything that I have?"

And even though Ynna had already used the name that she was able to read off his palm screen, she graciously said, "Yes, why don't you come with me to the ship and give me a little bit more information."

Moss was following them out as he felt the tug on his sleeve. He turned, thinking he was going to see Mr. Greene holding him back to say one final goodbye in case they weren't able to fix the water supply. Instead, he saw Millicent gazing up at him, her little hand holding the tip of his long-sleeved black shirt.

"My daddy says that you like these," she said and unfurled her other hand to reveal a tiny, pristinely folded origami tiger. It was crudely colored in orange and black and, presumably because she was the one who had colored it, green. "So, I did this for you."

Moss knelt so that he was on the same level as the girl and plucked the tiger out of her hand, gazing at it for a moment. "That's very sweet of you, thank you. Did you do it just now?"

"No, silly," the girl said and blew raspberries at him.

"We're taking a class together, with the grownups learning to fold origami and the kids doing the coloring," Mr. Greene explained. "I told her how I had an old friend who loves tigers and she said that if she ever met him, she wanted to give him the tiger."

Moss returned his gaze to the girl. "That's a really nice instinct."

"What's an instinct?" she asked.

"Something we do without thinking," Mr. Greene said and patted his daughter on the head. "He's saying you're really nice."

"I think most kids are nice," she observed. Moss smiled and couldn't help thinking about Derek and his deep seeded desire to see a world safe for the kids growing up in it.

"I think you're right," Moss said. "It's why your daddies and I want to give you a nice world."

"Okay," she said, and as though something else much more pressing occurred to her, she darted from the room. Moss stood and admired the tiger one more time before tucking it into his pocket.

"She's a really good kid," Moss told his old mentor.

"We like her," Mr. Greene said with a smile betraying that he loved that girl more than life itself.

"I'm so happy to see you guys this happy," Moss said, and he truly meant it. When he had run into Mr. Greene in Carcer City so long ago, Moss would never have believed that things could actually work out for them. But here they were.

"Thank you, Moss," Mr. Greene said. "And you? Are you happy?" And when he didn't answer after moment, Mr. Greene added, "I suppose it's a bit of a loaded question… given everything."

"Actually," Moss said, feeling a little smile cross his lips, "I am pretty happy. I proposed to Issy and she said yes. So, I have that to look forward to. Once this is all done."

"And when you say, 'this,' you are referring to the potential catastrophic poisoning of the entire population of the city?" Mr. Greene joked with a grim expression.

Moss shrugged. "Yeah, just that."

"I hope Brian's contact leads to something and that she can help you cure the city before it's too late," Mr. Greene said hopefully.

"Me too." Moss took a step forward to hug the older man. "It was really nice to see you."

"You too," Mr. Greene said with a smile. "Don't wait until the next catastrophic event to come visit."

"I won't. Plus, I need to come back and talk more about tigers with Millie."

Mr. Greene smiled at Moss in a way that he would've killed for when he was the man's employee. "She would love that. We all would."

"I promise." Moss smiled as he turned. "I won't be a stranger." As he cleared the door, he called back, "See ya, Millicent."

He heard a faint "Bye," as he stepped out into the street to find a bunch of gawkers standing around the dropship. He had to admit it looked a little bit peculiar sitting in the middle of the road in a residential neighborhood. Ynna and Issy were already inside and Brian was out front talking with the assembled crowd.

As he approached, a bunch of people turned and upon seeing him reacted as though he was a celebrity. They came running over to thank him for what he had done and what he was doing. Moss had never wanted to be famous or represent any kind of revolution, but years of being the most wanted had made him recognizable to most people.

"Thanks everyone," Moss said as he pushed through them to the ship. "Stay home, stay safe and stay away from the water for the time being. Keep your eye on the news and we will let you know when things return to normal."

He said it in a more commanding voice than he tended to use and it seemed to work. Everyone nodded and agreed. And he turned and caught Brian's eye as he pulled himself into the side of the ship.

"Brian, thanks for everything. You're hero to the city." Brian looked like he was going to burst with delight as everyone turned and hurried over to him.

Moss clipped himself into his seat and looked at Ynna. "You have what you need?"

"Think so," she said. "Let's just hope this is a lead worth following. Sounds like things are getting pretty grim in the city."

Moss nodded and the ship lifted as the drudge piloted them towards their destination.

Issy turned to Moss. "It was cute seeing you with them," she said. "I'll never forget how excited you were the first time Mr. Greene asked you out to dinner and how disappointed you were that it was just so he could try to convince you to take an advanced solar panel repair class."

"Feels like another lifetime."

"It was," Issy said. After a long time, she added, "Millicent was so cute."

"She really was," Ynna added from across the ship and as it began to descend almost as soon as it had taken off.

"That was quick," Moss said.

"I mean, he did say that he ran into her at the local grocery store," Issy observed but then fell silent as she saw Ynna's face. All the color had drained as she looked out the side window.

"Oh, fuck," Ynna muttered.

CHAPTER 4

As the ship set down once more in the street, the three disembarked to a ghastly visage. Children and their parents lay dead in the street under the spray of an open fire hydrant. They had undoubtedly been playing in it when the main had been poisoned and the parents had rushed to their children's side.

Moss had seen dead bodies. Escaping the gala in Africa, he had killed more people at once than he could count; but this was different. These were innocent people. These were children playing in the street and their families. Seeing all the bodies there, Moss couldn't believe what ThutoCo was doing. It was evil on a scale he hadn't thought possible until he felt the strange understanding Arthur Smith had left in his mind. It was a glimpse behind the curtain of an extremist – someone who didn't care how many people got hurt as long as their goals were met.

The three of them stared for a moment before Moss wrapped his arm around Issy and pulled her in the direction of the house. Ynna's whole body was shaking with rage and a tear rolled down her cheek. She looked homicidal and Moss knew she probably was.

Turning, she said through gritted teeth, "We have to end this."

As they trotted towards the house, Moss noticed how quiet it was. He wondered if anybody on the street when the event took place had fled. Or perhaps they were all in their own houses with empty water glasses next to their bodies.

A bird trilled and another answered as they made their way to the address Seti had acquired for them. Instinctively, they all pulled out weapons. Ynna was dressed in a version of the same intimidating attire that Moss had first met her in, but he and Issy were still disheveled wrecks in hastily donned clothes.

Issy seemed to be thinking the same thing as she hissed to Moss, "We really should have put on some armor."

"I'm sorry," Ynna said, though her mind seemed to be elsewhere. "I came to get you guys soon as I could and didn't really think about kitting you out. I didn't expect that we would get right into the action. Although, knowing us, I suppose I should have."

"It's okay," Moss said. "We are just going to find a scientist."

"Famous last words," Ynna joked as they made their way beyond the little rusted iron fence and over the plastic grass which encircled the home.

They stepped up the two stairs and Moss knocked as Ynna and Issy kept their weapons trained on the door. There was no answer and Moss felt his heart sink. This whole place felt post-apocalyptic and Moss was not confident that there was anybody left alive inside to help them.

He knocked again and again. There was no answer.

"Should I kick it in?" Moss asked

"I'd like to see you try," Ynna mocked.

"I have cybernetic legs!" Moss said and Issy was speaking simultaneously.

"She might just be at the store or something. We shouldn't kick her door in."

"I suppose you're right," Ynna said, rolling her eyes. "But I'm still not sure that your boyfriend could kick the door in even with robot legs."

"As soon as we get back to the safe house, I'm going to find a doo—" but he was cut off by the door shredding from the inside out from what had to be a bunch of guns fired at once. They all hit the ground as glass shattered and blurs moved overhead.

From the armor, they could tell it was more of the agents that ThutoCo had hired to trick Moss into thinking D2E was trying to kill them. They must have kept them on the payroll after Moss blew up their in-house armory.

Peering up through the now-obliterated door from his prone position, Moss could now see the agents. They wore heavy plate armor so dense, they looked like machines rather than men. Their feet shredded the faux grass as they crashed onto the ground and took off running. One of them had a person slumped over her shoulder.

"I guess we are on the right track," Moss yelled as the three jumped up to pursue the agents. They ran down the street in the opposite direction from the ship.

Moss and Ynna were in hot pursuit as Issy called, "I'll follow from the sky so we don't lose them," and raced to their ship.

It made Moss feel as he had when they played video games as children. Though she commended Moss on his instincts, she always knew exactly what to do so they wouldn't find themselves in a bad situation later. While Moss and Gibbs might rush headlong into a fight, Issy always had a plan.

As Issy sprinted in the other direction, Moss raised the weapon he had taken from the ship and began firing at one of the agents. Ynna did the same, letting off a volley with her machine gun. None of the bullets penetrated the armor, but the force of the burst knocked one of them to the ground.

Ynna fired another blast at the fallen agent and from point-blank range was able to shred through one of the joints. The agent screamed and then fell silent as the sound of their footsteps thumping up the street echoed off the houses.

The agent with the scientist over her shoulder shouted something to the other two and one of them turned, training his weapon directly at Moss and Ynna as he did so. Simultaneously, they jumped left and right to avoid incoming fire. Ynna landed behind a metal garbage can while Moss took cover behind a bush that immediately erupted into a torrent of bullets and leaves.

As the world around Moss exploded, Ynna jumped up and charged the agent. By the time he turned to take her on, she was already upon him, leaping into the air and forcing him to the ground. She grabbed the top of the chest plate and used force to bring him down, pressing the muzzle of her rifle into the gap at his neck and firing as they fell. Wasting no time, she kept running after the other two as Moss emerged from behind the bush and hurried to catch up.

His cybernetic legs made quick work of it. He was beside her as they rounded the corner and saw the lead agent loading the scientist onto the back of a flighted bike. The other agent took a few shots to keep them from following and in a moment they were off.

Coming back out from around the corner they had ducked behind for cover, Moss and Ynna grabbed the two remaining bikes. Moss had never flown one and he tried to start the engine by pressing the button he assumed would turn the thing on. It did not.

Looking up, Moss saw Ynna staring at him angrily and waving him over to jump on the back of her bike. She revved the engine and they were off, lurching into the sky as Moss hung on for dear life. The city blurred around them and the wind whipped through their hair as they pursued the agents between buildings. They tilted and turned, banking hard as they chased them past an apartment complex where people were yelling and screaming as the vehicle zipped by.

Moss hadn't realized the bikes could go this fast and he could barely keep his eyes open as Ynna picked up speed to close in on the agents.

"Fucking shoot them!" she shouted; the words barely audible.

Moss raised his hand, the force of the airflow making it nearly impossible. Squinting, he tried to aim, but when he fired a shot, it went well wide.

The second agent fired back over her shoulder and Ynna had to barrel roll out of the path of the incoming fire. Her hair lashed Moss's face as his stomach lurched and he gripped her hard. When they evened out, he tried to fire again but missed again.

"Try to get closer!" he screamed in her ear, but as she accelerated, he immediately regretted his words. The sound of wind and buildings whipping by was all he could hear as they closed in.

The lead agent turned her bike and led the chase into a narrow alley, lined with buildings so old they hunched like old people's backs toward one another. Small balconies, air-conditioning units, delivery drones and clotheslines made the pathway a gauntlet, and Ynna had to swerve and drop to keep moving forward. With each move, Moss felt more like he was going to vomit and wished that he had just stayed on the ground. But he was here and he would do his best.

Raising his weapon, he took a few more shots, and this time struck the bike. Coolant began to stream from the side of the thing and Moss watched as it began to shudder. The agent was furiously tapping the control screen, trying to adjust and correct before the bike spun out of control. Doing this caused him to slow enough that Ynna was able to catch up. The agent turned to see that they were upon him, but by the time he raised his weapon to shoot, Moss was already firing the volley.

The bike spun out of control and careened towards the ground, crunching against the cement and exploding in a bright flash of plastic and metal. Ynna gunned it once again, propelling them forward at a sickening speed to catch the lead agent. From one of the windows of a nearby building, a child cried something before shooting at them with the foam dart from a toy gun. Unlike all the real bullets the agents had fired at them, the little yellow dart made contact, hitting Moss in the shoulder before disappearing in a flash as they zipped away. Moss couldn't help but laugh.

They closed in and sensing them the lead agent looked over her shoulder before turning back and rocketing toward the ground. Ynna sank the bike's nose toward the ground. Moss held on for dear life and watched as the ground rushed up to meet them. She revved the thrusters just before hitting the cement and blasted forward, heading up the street between the traffic.

Sliding left and right and dodging cars, the two bikes zipped forward. The mathematical traffic of self-driving cars didn't slow or stop as the two bikes flew through it. The agent approached a series of trucks and jumped her bike, firing the engine to zoom over the vehicles. Moss pulled himself together enough to lift the weapon but Ynna slapped it away.

"We both know you'll hit the fucking scientist," she called, and Moss had to admit that she was probably right.

The woman's unconscious body was slumped over the back of the bike, thrashing against the come-alongs that kept her lashed to the back. Her legs and arms flopped limply as the bike hurtled up the street.

The commotion created by the moving cars and the city streets beneath them seemed to distract the agent, and Ynna was able to pull their bike up close. To Moss's horror, she began to shift her body, moving her legs up onto the body of the bike.

He knew what she intended to do and he swallowed hard as he slid forward. He moved under her and put his hands on the control sticks as she crouched on the metal body and then jumped. Moss took control of a rocketing vehicle he had never driven before as she moved through the air, pulling out her nanoblade.

Though Moss could not see through the helmet of the agent, he could imagine the shock written on her face as Ynna flew onto the bike. Landing on the nose of the thing, she threw the blade through the ropes tethering the captured woman to the machine. As the bike was propelled downward, the scientist was catapulted into the air. Moss's heart stopped and his eyes went wide as he watched her limp body fly upwards.

The dropship suddenly appeared, banked, and from the open side door Issy grabbed the scientist and pulled her on board. It was the most amazing series of events Moss had ever seen and he turned back to the road just in time to avoid crashing into an ADrone displaying a commercial for Spuck Nuggets.

The agent had evened out her bike and was groping back with one arm to grab the nanoblade from where it had sunk into the metal. Ynna reached for the machine gun clipped to her belt, but as soon as she pulled it free, the agent knocked it from her hand before moving to reach for the blade again. Ynna had her back to the street and was blocking the view of the already distracted agent, so she didn't see the street pole that collected real-time traffic images.

Moss turned the sticks, horrified by how reactive the controls were, and his own bike went crashing into the side of the other; but it did the job. Both bikes moved out of the way just in time to avoid slamming into the pole. Moss tried to pull his bike away, it's twisted metal had snagged on the other bike and he used the opportunity to reach back and pull the nanoblade free.

He slid it out as the agent reset an arm to punch Moss in the face. He ducked, and the force of the movement, loosing the bikes from one another and his went flying across the street, the auto-correctors thrusting off the left-hand side to keep him from crashing into a building.

He looked up to see the agent and Ynna on the other bike, struggling and punching each another, as the bike continued to zip forward. Ynna turned for the briefest of moments and Moss thought he saw her wink at him. His mouth formed a perfect circle in amazement as he watched Ynna jump from the nose of the bike and spin over the head of the agent, coming down on the rear of the vehicle.

With her cybernetic hand, she gripped the back of the bike and the entire vehicle spun head over heels. The agent was thrown free, flying through the air before slamming into the ground. The armor was so heavy that she cracked the street and Moss didn't think there was any way she could survive the impact.

As the back of the bike circled back upward, Ynna let go and was thrown upward, flying through the air like a superhero as the dropship turned sidelong. Moss was sure she was going to land effortlessly through the open door, but her body was moving so fast that she crashed into Issy, who had been standing there hoping to catch her. The two women were thrown to the floor of the dropship as Moss killed the engine of his bike.

Parking on the sidewalk, he stepped off the bike, happier to be on flat earth than he could remember being. But his body seemed to believe it was still moving at high speeds and he couldn't stay upright, falling to his knees and placing his palms flat on the pavement. Soon, he was the centre of an excited commotion and watched as some people began to snap photos.

The dropship lowered right next to him as Ynna and Issy pulled themselves together, asking one another if they were all right. Moss got to his feet and Issy extended a hand, helping him into the dropship as the drudge lifted it skyward.

Rubbing her sore body, Ynna hooked a thumb at the scientist and said, "She'd better be worth it."

Surprising all of them, the scientist said groggily, "I am."

CHAPTER 5

"You know who we are?" Moss asked as the ship drifted slowly over the city.

There was a time when they would've been shot out of the sky by any Carcer patrol that saw them, but now they could fly anywhere they wanted to without fear of destruction.

The woman looked at them shakily. Having been taken from her home, she wasn't dressed like a scientist. She was in simple sweatpants and an oversized hoodie bearing the brand logo of a university. Her hair was graying from the roots in a way that suggested she didn't keep up with her dyeing it. Obviously haggard from everything that had just happened to her, she looked exhausted; but her eyes were bright and showed no trace of fear.

"Took you long enough," she said.

"What's that?" Ynna asked.

"Figured you would come find me the moment I gave Brian my number," she said, scrunching her face up in a way that suggested she was annoyed with them.

"Pretty cryptic communication, if you ask me," Ynna snapped back. "Also, we did just save your ass."

"Wouldn't have needed saving if you came for me in the first place," the woman said, and Moss could tell she wouldn't take shit from anyone.

Ynna was opening her mouth to say something invariably nasty, so Moss spoke quickly.

"Seems we got off on the wrong foot but we're all on the same team, so let's try this again." He extended a hand across the belly of the ship and said, "Hi, I'm Moss. It's good to meet you."

"Carl," the woman said, "a pleasure." Hands were shaken all around, but Moss could tell Carl and Ynna had an instant dislike of one another. "So, you're here about the water?"

"We are, but first I have to ask, is your child all right?" Ynna asked and Moss was surprised.

Carl clearly was too, but she smiled and said, "Yes, she's with my ex and we filter everything for this very reason. Though I'm sure he's giving her nothing but chocolate milk just to be safe…and win brownie points with her."

"Good," Moss muttered, still a bit confused. "But, yes, we're here about the water. Can you help us?"

Carl looked at him in annoyance. "Of course I can! Haven't you read any of my articles?"

Moss looked at Issy and Ynna, who both shook their heads, and Carl watched this in dismay. "What are you people doing?"

"We're trying to save the fucking world!" Ynna snapped.

"Better late than never," Carl muttered under her breath.

"Precisely," Moss said. "Tell us what we would have read in the articles."

Carl sighed theatrically but the hint of a smile crossed her lips, as she was clearly excited to lecture them.

"I was fired from ThutoCo because, during the course of my work, I was able to synthesize a cure to what we, in-house, called the Romero Spore Disease or RSD.

"I had my suspicions about the genesis of the disease and the nature of curing it, so I went public with my information. Well, public isn't quite the right word. I went internally public, which was my mistake. I learned pretty quickly that ThutoCo did not, in fact, want to cure RSD or let it be known that we had a cure at all. Obviously, I now know that they had cured it long before I ever fabricated a solution, but c'est la vie.

"Anyway, after going internally public with my finding, I found myself on the street. BurbSec waited until I was in the shower to break into my hex so I got the added indignity of being dragged through the entire burb naked before being interrogated.

"The problem for them was that I had sent that email. If I had sent one just to my boss, they could've disappeared me quietly; but because I made a stink, they couldn't just kill me. Instead, they destroyed all my research and forced me on the first shuttle into the city. I promise you, naked and alone is not how you want to enter B.A. City for your first time, but it *can* land you a husband, even if he's the type you don't want to stay with once you've figured life out.,

"So, I set about trying to make my research known to the world. I've spent nearly all my time trying to get the word out. I mean," and she let out a disgusted laugh, "I've warned everyone for years that this day would come. Nobody listened. Apparently, not even the people who should have."

"I'm sorry, we didn't know," Moss said.

Carl turned red eyes on Moss. "You should have!"

He could see this woman's pain. He could sense how hard it had been for her to screaming the truth for years, knowing nobody was listening. When people started dropping this morning, her heart must have broken.

"I truly am sorry. We are not some vast network. We are just a few people trying to fight as hard as we can."

"That may be the case, but a lot of people are dying because you never heard me. I am Cassandra watching the fall of Troy," Carl said softly.

"No," Moss told her. "The horse may be within the walls, but we are listening now and we can stop this. What do you need from us?"

From under the developing bruises, a small smile crossed her lips. "I need a lab."

Then, a smile crossed Moss's.

"I never thought I would see you again," Gil said. "Not in real life anyway."

He ran over and passionately shook Moss's hand until Moss just pulled him in for a hug. They had only met once and briefly, but his time at The Conservation had a deep impact on Moss.

"It's good to see you," Moss said and he truly meant it. "This is my fiancée Issy, this is Ynna and this is…"

"Carl!" Gil exclaimed, racing over to shake her hand. "We follow your updates daily and I am so happy to have you here. Our people will be so excited to meet you. A whistleblower who bucked the system and survived — it's quite a thing."

"Thank you!" Carl said excitedly, "It's good to be among people who appreciate my work."

"We have wanted to contact you for so long but knew it would imperil us both," Gil told her.

"Of course," she said. "I understand. But I am here now, so let's get to work."

Gil nodded and waved in the direction of a man in a lab coat. Carl nodded and joined him as Gil turned to Moss, Ynna and Issy.

"Can I offer you all some coffee? The beans were grown here in dirt specially designed to grow coffee. You can taste the difference, I promise you."

Moss grinned. "I would love that!"

"Actually," Ynna said a bit sheepishly, "Is there a restroom I could use?"

"Honestly, I could pee, too," Issy admitted.

Gil smiled graciously. "Naturally," he said and pointed them to a door. "Out that door, down the hall, to the left. Why don't you two meet Moss and me in the cafeteria upstairs? There will be a map across from the restroom, but if you follow any staircase up, you should be able to spot us."

Issy smiled and thanked him, but Ynna took off in a hurry.

Once the two men were alone in the room, Gil smiled at Moss and said, "Shall we?"

"Let's shall," Moss said and followed Gil out of the concrete substructure and up into the building itself.

The smell of wet earth, damp air and wildlife filled his nostrils as he stepped out onto the metal pathway over the pools of water below. A glass rotunda in the middle with a jungle inside glistened and colorful birds flew overhead. In a strange way, Moss felt like he was home. Being out in proper nature had made him nervous and was overwhelming, but this contained wilderness was perfect for him. The exact blend of natural and synthetic that he craved. Of course, Issy had been right about him. This was where he wanted to be, needed to be.

"I love the way you look around when you're here," Gil observed, following Moss's eyes to the sloth sleeping in a tree just over the door to the cafeteria. "I sometimes forget, but not when you are here."

"How could you forget?" Moss asked, sincerely perplexed as he looked beneath his feet to watch a mola mola swim by.

Gil chuckled, pushing the door to the cafeteria open. "It's like any job. Even if it is a passion, it's still a job. I'm sure there are days that you would rather not have to hero around or whatever it is that you do."

"Touché," Moss said, but he was distracted by one of the walls.

It was entirely made of glass and contained an ant colony. As if carried by magic, Moss drifted over to watch the millions of creatures go diligently about their business. It was mesmerizing; as those on the surface brought leaves below, others continued to build their nest and still more tended to the queen. It was remarkable and Moss didn't know how long he had been standing there before Gil appeared beside him with the trays.

"Didn't know what you might like so I got you a salad with grilled chicken," Gil said. Moss's face must've registered his disappointment, because the man added, "We should all eat more greens. It's good for us."

"Fine," Moss grumbled, thinking about Stan as he followed Gil to a long plastic table with attached bench seating. "I had a friend who used to tell me that all the time, too. Told me everything I know about food. Made my culinary education his life's quest. Always tried to get us to eat healthier."

"Good man," Gil observed and it reminded Moss that he needed to follow up on a call. After a while, Gil said, "Sounds as if the city's a disaster."

"Yup," Moss agreed. "Poisoning people's drinking water will do that."

"At least they only poisoned the water," Gil said.

It took Moss a moment, but he soon realized that what Gil was saying was true. "Sure, it's certainly better than the previous iteration."

"After our talk," Gil said, "we started to run a lot of models to get geared up for the possible eventuality of attempting reintroduction and repopulation. This plan will never look like what it did before, but between what's left in the untouched spaces and the samples we have here, we might be able to get back to some semblance of earth as it should be."

"That's remarkable," Moss said. "I can't imagine this fight even being worth it without you guys."

Gil looked floored by the comment. "That's quite a thing to say."

"I mean it," Moss said. "And... I've been thinking about my future..."

"Hey," a tiny voice said. "I know you."

Moss turned to see Gil's daughter. "Hi, Amy," he said, surprised by how much bigger she was than the last time he'd seen her. "You kids keep growing up."

"Everything is just growing up," Amy observed. She slid next to her dad and plucked a piece of chicken off his salad.

"I suppose that's true," Moss said.

A grim expression crossed Amy's face. "Sorry to hear about Anders."

"Me too," Moss said. "I know you guys had a special thing."

"He was always nice to me and I loved the presents he brought me, but his death was really just a loss for the galaxy. Did he ever tell you about his adventures in space?" she asked with wonder in her eyes.

"Not as much as I would've liked." Moss realized the truth of it as the words left his lips. "He was the kind of person who made space for other people to talk about their problems more than he ever talked about his own."

"He was a good man like that," Gil said, and Moss could hear the emotion in his voice.

"He was the type of guy everyone should try to be like," Amy said and Moss looked at her with wonderment. Though she was probably only twice as old as Millicent, she seemed like an adult. Moss couldn't help but smile.

"You know," Moss said, feeling emotions well within himself as well, "I think the world is in good hands with your generation."

"Couldn't be any worse than yours," Amy said with a smirk. "So, obviously, it would have to be better."

"Who's this?" Moss heard Issy's voice from over his shoulder.

"Woah," Amy remarked as the two women walked over. "You're both so beautiful."

Moss turned to see Issy and Ynna both blush at the girl's comment. "Well, thank you…?"

"Amy," she announced, looking down at her drab khakis with visible insecurities.

"Well, thank you, Amy. And you are cute as a button in your uniform," Issy said, having caught the look.

Ynna seemed to be in some far-off place and didn't speak as she sat down at the table.

"So, you guys are like, rebel fighters?" Amy asked of the women.

"I never really thought of myself that way," Issy admitted with a broad smile, "but, yeah, kinda. My friend Ynna, here, just jumped from the side of a hover bike into a spaceship."

Amy's face brightened. "No way!"

"It's true," Ynna said but her face showed worry and she looked at Gil. "Do you… run all kinds of tests here?"

Gil gave Ynna kindly smile. "We do," he told her. "I can have us run whatever kind of test you need."

He didn't have to be told it was urgent, and simply stood and gestured for Ynna to follow him. "You mind keeping an eye on these two?" he asked Amy.

"It'll cost you one salad," she told him.

He chuckled. "Deal," he said and he guided Ynna out the door.

Moss turned and gave Issy a questioning look. She smiled. "It's exactly what you think," she whispered and Moss felt his heart fill.

Turning to look back at Amy, he said, "The future of the world really is going to be in good hands."

CHAPTER 6

"Had to have us fly all the way out here?" Gibbs asked as he met Moss in the underbelly of The Conservation. "Guess you just wanted to show us how much you love this place?"

"Wish it were just that," Moss said with a laugh. "Actually, we have a scientist who is currently working with the team here to synthesize a cure for the poison in the water."

"Oh, snap," Patchwork said as he sidled up next to Gibbs. "You have been getting after it."

"That we have," Moss said. Judy was right behind the two and Moss winked at them before saying, "Come on, I can't wait to show you this place."

He led them upstairs, forcing them to listen as he talked at length about the work the lab was doing and the wildlife species the scientists were looking at. Patchwork seemed genuinely interested and Judy put on a brave face, but Gibbs had heard it all before. He made Moss watch countless movies and lectured him throughout, but always got a bit bored when Moss made him watch wildlife documentaries that his parents had kept on drives in a shoebox. The BurbNet didn't really show anything about the outside world.

Moss smiled to himself as they neared the little side room beside the lab and he turned and said, "Gibbs, you're gonna love this!"

Gibbs rolled his eyes. "I love you, man, but this stuff just doesn't do it for me."

"This one might," he said as he swung the door open, revealing Ynna standing in the middle of the room with a piece of paper.

Gibbs immediately knew that something was off about the whole situation, looking from Moss to Ynna with suspicion. Tears then formed in Gibbs's eyes and Moss could tell the rest of the world fell away. It was just him and Ynna in the room.

Issy came over from the corner of the room and held Moss's hand. It felt like such an intimate moment to be a part of, but Ynna had said she knew Gibbs well enough to know he would like an audience.

As he got close, Gibbs reached out for the piece of paper in her hand but she withdrew it and said, "I threw up when I got here."

Moss could see his friend's shoulders shake as he already was starting to cry, but he simply said, "Because you had to listen to Moss talk about this place for so long?"

Ynna laughed and began to cry as well. "But I was nervous because I had just done all this crazy fighting stuff and I didn't know... well... anyway..." and she thrust the paper against his chest. He didn't have to read it to know what it said. He wrapped her in his arms and they both began sobbing hard as their friends gathered around them.

Through tears of joy, Ynna said, "Samuel Gibson the fourth."

Laughing, Gibbs said, "Only if it's a girl."

After several minutes of tearful celebration, Judy turned to Moss and said, "Those two as parents..."

Moss chuckled. "I know, it's gonna be some kind of ass-kicking nerd."

"So.... Pretty much you?" Judy mocked and Moss nearly spit out his drink with laughter

"Yeah," he said, "pretty much."

They smiled and, once again, though they were happy for their friends, Moss knew Judy lamented that it wasn't them. He put his hand on their back and offered, "You are one of the best friends I could ever have hoped for." It wasn't much but it was what he felt and hoped it was something.

They looked up at him with gratitude written all over their face and the permanent sadness in their eyes and said, "You're not too bad, yourself... once you get to know you."

"Awww, that's the nicest thing you've ever said to me," Moss said and they punched him playfully but hard on the shoulder. "Also!" he said excitedly, "I can finally repay the favor of you introducing me to coffee."

"Really?" Judy said with a little smirk. "Might I remind you that when I gave you that coffee the first time you said–"

"Yeah, yeah, yeah," Moss said, rolling his eyes. "That's entirely beside the point. But they grow coffee beans here and when you try what they produce, you will realize we've been drinking swill for our entire lives."

He walked them over to the little table in the corner that Gil had set up with drinks and he poured himself and Judy cups from the carafe.

"Oh, shit!" Judy exclaimed as the liquid touch their lips. "You really weren't kidding."

"I know, right?" he said as he took another step, savoring the flavor.

"It's remarkable," Judy said, staring into their cup, lost in thought for a moment.

"It's better than–" Moss began.

"Better than what?" Issy said and Moss turned to see her standing behind him. "Don't try to get out of it, I know what you were gonna say."

"Try it and you'll understand," Moss said, offering her the cup.

"You know I don't drink coffee," she said and smirked before adding, "I guess I'm just stuck with sex."

"And with him, you poor thing," Judy said, winking at Issy.

She groaned. "I know, what's even the point?" she said with a laugh and then turned to look at Moss seriously. "You should go congratulate your friend."

"Okay, Mom," Moss whined like a petulant child and Issy immediately put her palm on his face, turning and tilting him towards his friends and giving him a slight shove. Smiling, he turned and walked toward Gibbs and Ynna who were still beaming. They both turned and looked up at him with misty eyes. "Congrats, you guys."

"Thanks," they both said in unison and turned to give him a hug.

"Okay," Ynna said seriously. "I have to ask, did he tell you?"

Moss shook his head. "Did who tell me what?"

"Well, no shit," Ynna said, turning to Gibbs and holding up her hand which he promptly high-fived. "I was sure he was going to tell you we were trying."

While stunned that he hadn't, Moss simply said, "Nope, not a peep."

"I'm really so impressed," Ynna said.

"Honestly, I am too," Moss agreed. "So, Ynna, guess this means you'll be taking a backseat for a minute?"

Her face hardened and she said, "Yes. You fucking bubs will be the ones to take down ThutoCo once and for all, but it doesn't mean I'll be sitting around with my feet up. I can still work and lead. I just won't be able to, you know, get in gunfights."

As she said the last part, Moss was surprised that she didn't sound angry. He could tell that while she was mad that she didn't get to be part of the action, she was too happy to care. That, more than anything, made him happy for her.

"Ynna, you have more leadership in your little finger than most people have in their entire bodies. We couldn't do anything without you and would be nowhere without you. I would be dead ten times over."

"And me, like, twenty," Gibbs interjected.

"Seriously, Ynna, it won't matter if you're not in the actual building with us or getting shot at or whatever. You are this entire revolution and always have been," Moss said.

Her face scrunched as she tried to hold back tears but she let them come saying, "Thanks   This is all just the hormones, okay?"

"You're no less tough for crying," Gibbs told her.

She sniffled, chuckled and said, "*You* would say that." Turning to Moss, she said, "You better fucking keep him alive."

"I would literally die before letting anything happen to him," Moss said sincerely and Ynna nodded. "Plus," he said and turned to look at Issy still talking to Judy, "we all know it's going to be her who keeps us both alive."

"She always has," Gibbs observed.

"Got that right," Moss said.

"It still blows my mind that you guys have known each other your whole lives," Ynna said. "It's really cool. I hope our kid has lifelong friends, too."

"Yeah, but maybe they won't have to go to war alongside them," Gibbs said, already sounding like a nervous father.

Moss continued to stare at Issy from across the room. He was so happy to have her back in his life and so happy about the future they were going to build together. He wanted to have the moment that his friends were having right now with her. He wanted to feel happy and safe and free.

"Anyone in here named Moss?" a voice said from across the room, and he turned to see an elderly man sticking his head in the door. Moss raised a hand in greeting and walked over. "A woman by the name of Carl asked to speak with you," the man whispered at Moss's approach.

"Thank you," he said and turned back to the room. "Congrats again, you guys," he called and added, "I'll be right back."

Moss followed the man back out into the open space. He moved very slowly, which was fine with Moss, because it meant that he could stop and admire all the wildlife. He gawked as butterflies fluttered past, watched as a lizard licked its own eyeball and marveled at the little netted off area with gigantic bats hanging upside down. As much as he explored the space, he knew there was so much more that he hadn't seen and was so excited to one day just walk freely through it all. Gil had told him that it was much larger than he had any concept of and that, with some training, he could even swim in the pools with the ocean life.

The old man guided him into a small conference room where Carl was now dressed per title – wearing a lab coat with glasses propped on her head, pushing her hair back. The bruises had developed into dark purple and yellow on her face but the cuts had been mended and she seemed in good spirits.

"This place is miraculous," she said as Moss into the room.

"I couldn't agree more!" Moss said. "Have you seen all the wildlife they have here?"

"No, but have you seen all the lab equipment they have?"

"We also have one of the most extensive libraries remaining on the planet," the old man added as both Moss and Carl turned to him.

"Thank you, Bill," Carl said, trying not to sound patronizing but failing. The old man took the hint and shuffled from the room. Carl grimaced to herself. "Shoot, I really didn't want to make him feel bad."

"I'm sure he'll get over it," Moss said.

"Him getting over it doesn't make me feel any better about having done it," Carl said, furrowing her brows and then wincing at the pain. "Anyway, we've already begun synthesizing the antidote."

"Holy shit, that was fast," Moss said, sincerely impressed.

"Well, if you had read my blog, you would've known that I already had the formula. I just needed somewhere to actually produce it. And it turns out, you can't get the kind of supplies I needed in your kid's chemistry set."

Moss felt his face fall flat. "Listen, I really appreciate what you're doing for us, but you kinda have to drop the attitude. I'm not your enemy."

"Not being my enemy doesn't make you my friend either. We may both be working towards the same goal, but I've been suffering in silence and could have prevented a lot of death if you guys had just found the time to listen," she said.

That was what it was about. "Listen," he said, looking her right in the eyes. "It wasn't your fault that people died today. ThutoCo poisoned the water, not you. You're working to cure it and you're working as quickly as you can. You cannot blame yourself for what somebody else did."

"You can if you had the means to prevent it," she snapped back, the guilt not shaking loose. Moss knew the feeling well.

"That's just it," he said. "You didn't have the means to stop it. You couldn't have kept the water treatment plant safe from ThutoCo agents and you couldn't have known that they were going to do this today. You have to stop beating yourself up and start feeling good about what you're doing now." He pointed through the window to the room of lab techs and machines working away to create the antidote she had formulated.

"Listen, man, I'm sure this motivational shit works on your friends, but I don't know you and I don't have to feel anyway except how I want to feel, got me?"

Moss was surprised. His heart-to-heart talks with his friends did tend to make them feel better and he was disappointed that it wasn't working on her. But he wasn't going to waste any more time on it.

"Fair enough," he said. "So, what do we need to know?"

She handed him a coat, boot covers, goggles and gloves, which he put on before they entered the lab. As they walked in, she gestured to a large vat in the corner with robotic arms working away at adding certain amounts of chemicals to the mixture.

Moss blinked and turned to her in surprise. "We need to transport all that?"

"Oh, it'll be a lot more than that," Carl said, seemingly shocked by his surprise. "It's an entire city's water supply that needs to be treated. This needs to be added at multiple points to ensure that nothing is missed. What'd you expect?"

Moss shrugged and shook his head. "I don't know. Like a little vial or something."

"Well, I'm sorry, that's not really how science works."

"Right," Moss sighed. "All right, tell me what I need to do."

CHAPTER 7

"Nervous?" Gibbs asked.

"Weirdly, I am," Moss admitted as he and his friend stood in the center of their subterranean lair in an old subway station. The rest of the crew were stationed in various spots around the hideout, just in case.

"Me too." Gibbs nervously ran his hands along the length of the rifle hanging from his shoulder.

Then they heard it. The sound of boots marching down the staircase. One by one, the Carcer wardens began to appear. There were so many of them, all in black fatigues and armor; all wearing weapons of different sorts and helmets to cover their faces. They began falling in on either side of Moss and Gibbs before clicking their heels and turning to form shoulder-to-shoulder columns.

It was so surreal that Moss almost couldn't handle it. These men and women had been out to kill him for so long. He had been their top priority, the most valuable bounty on earth, and now here they were. Watching them file in, his hand began to shake despite his brain telling it to stop. The line stopped at the bottom of the stairs and the wardens stood at perfect attention.

It was nearly silent in the room except for the sound of slow breaths hissing from the wardens' helmets. Moss could feel his heartbeat in his throat as one more set of footfalls clomped down the stairs. Soon, the unmistakable visage of Todd Davis appeared at the bottom of the stairs. Seeing him made Moss smile. The chief executive officer and president of the Carcer Corporation board was dressed in a perfectly tailored suit that nonetheless appeared militaristic. It was black with red trim and bore the handcuffed scorpion pincers logo of the company on its lapel.

Todd also carried a cane, which he clicked as he strode between the row of wardens. "Formerly classified terrorist Moss," Todd announced as he walked the line.

"Newly minted head of the world's largest private military firm," Moss answered back.

Todd stopped directly in front of Moss and smiled. In that moment, despite the mask, Moss could see Puck's eyes.

"It's good to see *you*," Moss told him.

"It's good to be seen," Puck said softly from beneath his guise. He then announced, "You were once the most hunted man in our company's history, and now you will be our largest paycheck."

"Will your people be able to work with me?" Moss matched Puck's volume. This entire show was being put on for the wardens.

"We never had a problem with you," Todd Davis, for all intents and purposes, announced. "Our jobs are never personal; they are strictly business. We are as happy to work with you as we would have been to work with those you outbid. We are professionals."

At the last word, all the wardens stomped their left feet simultaneously. It was exactly the sign Moss needed to see, proof that these men and women had always been chasing money. Warden Ninety-Nine had been an outlier. It had become personal for him, but the rest of these people were simply hired thugs with better armor. They were the same as the agents against which Moss would use them.

"Fall out!" Todd demanded of his soldiers and all the wardens made a show of marching back upstairs, just as they did coming downstairs. One stayed behind, the number one written on her shoulders.

She walked over and said, "Sir?"

"Dismissed, One," he said and got only a nod in response before the woman joined her compatriots upstairs.

Once they were alone, Gibbs said, "Well, that was weird."

"Your performance was but momentary," Puck, now behaving as himself, said. "Imagine doing this your whole life and with your life on the line."

"Maybe you forgot. We did," Moss told him.

"Pish posh, things that happened before we met don't count," Puck said with a fanciful wave of his hand.

Moss laughed and embraced the man quickly. "Though I can't imagine why, I have missed you."

"I feel as though I'm supposed to say I have missed you too and, while I have, being the head of an evil mega-corporation does have its benefits. I flew Curtis out here and he and his entire family now have an estate on my compound," Puck said as he ran his fingers down the front of his suit. He saw Moss trying to place the name and said, "He was my clothier in Cape City."

"Oh," Moss said, his memory jogged. "I would never have remembered him."

"I won't tell him," Puck said with a wink.

Moss shrugged. "I don't know that I would care if you did..."

"Oh, what a prick," Puck said and tapped his cane against the tile floor.

"You always seem to bring it out of me," Moss chuckled.

"That I do," Puck said without hesitation. "It was my sister for whom you saved your good half… or your lower half, at any rate."

Gibbs laughed so loudly that the sound echoed through the entire station.

Moss shook his head and Puck smirked from ear to ear. "I'm sorry, old chum, it was just so easy and I so infrequently get to be myself these days."

"Don't worry about it," Moss said, but any mention of Irene always gave him complicated feelings. He'd only known the real woman for a few minutes, but in that time had watched her die for no good reason. It still hurt to think about.

"So, what precisely can we do for you?" Puck asked. "There are only a very few places we can go without the citizenry throwing rocks or tomatoes or air-conditioners at us."

Gibbs guffawed. "Air-conditioners?"

Puck turned a very serious face on him. "Yes."

"We don't need your help with anything in the city proper," Moss said. "We just need more men to help us secure the water treatment plant."

"Why not just use your people?" Puck asked.

"Because I miss you so desperately and wanted to see you," Moss said, batting his eyelashes at Puck.

"If only that were the case," Puck snorted.

"All of our people are busy helping the citizenry of the city. We are going to be getting smaller doses of the antidote as injectables to them to help with on-the-ground treatment," Moss told him. "Everyone has their own reasons for being here, but one thing we all share is a desire to help the people of the city and I'm happy to let your people die so that mine can help others."

Puck nodded but his face looked pained. "You know, now that I'm on the inside and have come to know many of the people who work at the Carcer Corporation, I must say —"

"Nope!" Gibbs did not let him finish and held up a hand. "We're not interested in any of that 'the SS were just following orders' shit."

"I understand," Puck said.

"Before we get the show on the road, you want to say hi to everybody else?" Moss asked.

Puck smiled and said, "Of course. Couldn't come all this way and not see the merry band of scalawags."

"Pretty sure we never agreed to that name," Moss said with a chuckle as he turned to lead Puck to where the rest were staying.

As they walked, Puck whispered in Moss's ear, "I dealt with that other thing too."

Moss nodded. "Thank you," he whispered back, "I will follow up on that after."

"Certainly," Puck said, clapping him on the back. Then, as they were walking down the narrow passageway, he grew serious and said, "I'm sorry, too."

"Why?" Moss said. "You've been doing a remarkable job."

"I should've just killed Arthur Smith but the moment got the better of me."

He looked away, abashed, and while Gibbs kept walking, Moss stepped in front of Puck and said, "Don't do that to yourself. You got to beat the shit out of a bad person but also didn't blow your cover so badly that you got thrown out of the company. We still have you installed at the head of Carcer and that's one hell of a thing.

"I know you haven't been able to free up your soldiers to help us as much as you would've liked, but being here now is exactly what we need, when we need. Sure, you could've killed Arthur, but it wouldn't have stopped ThutoCo. You would've gotten yourself killed *and* the AIC would have been able to use it to rally supporters."

"Yes," Puck said thoughtfully, "I suppose that is true. But I still lament my actions. Perhaps I could have worked harder to keep our spot on the AIC, take them down from the inside."

Moss shook his head. "We had a man on the inside. Didn't really matter, ultimately. You've done great, Puck, and don't forget it. You were tasked with an impossible job and have risen to the occasion. Nobody could have done what you've done and don't think we will ever forget it. Also, and not for nothing, but we will need you soon, too."

"How do you mean?"

"If we take down all the megas there will likely be chaos and we may need you," Moss explained, having thought a lot about what they were going to do if they managed to actually succeed.

"I don't expect the appearance of Carcer officers back on the streets is going to send the message you might hope," Puck said, tilting his head.

Moss laughed. "No, I don't imagine it would," he said with a smile. "But I wasn't thinking that so much as some help mopping up. All these companies have their own private armies or security forces and, while we've dealt with ThutoCo's, there will still be more fight ahead."

"The Night Crystal still has a good number of troops and I have some protecting our buildings around the city, but most of the soldiers have been reallocated. I'll start bringing them back quietly so as not to arouse any suspicions," Puck said.

"Good," Moss said. "Once we start taking the fight to them, we need to have our ducks in a row, or everything is gonna fall apart."

Puck looked Moss over in a peculiar way and let out a little exhalation of approval. "You've come a long way."

"Thank you," Moss said.

"I always thought it would be Ynna who stepped up once Sandra perished, but it seems that you are doing a cracking job here and being wise by looking to the future."

Moss chuckled. "Actually, she does get to be looking to the future in a different way."

"Oh, truly?" Puck said, holding his hands over his heart in excitement. "That is wonderful news. I'm so happy to have something to look forward to that isn't death and destruction."

"That makes two of us," Moss said. "On both counts."

"Pardon?"

"I always figured Ynna as the leader, too," Moss admitted.

"Humility is a leadership trait in its own right," Puck advised.

Moss smiled. "I'll take that in the spirit it was intended."

"Do," Puck said.

"Come on, friend, I want to buy you a drink."

"Now, my dear boy, you're speaking my language."

CHAPTER 8

It had taken a while for everyone to get used to Puck's new face, but they all came around eventually and had a really nice night catching up with their old friend.

Eventually, they received word from Carl that the antidote was ready, and the conversation had to come to a close. As they were gearing up to leave, Gil grabbed Moss's arm. "There is a place for you here, always," he said seriously.

Mass had assumed they would take him, but there was something about being told outright that filled his heart with joy.

"Thank you," Moss said.

Gil looked at him with one side of his lip turned up slightly.

"No," he said, "thank you. For all you have done and will do. There could have been any number of people who took on the companies but it was you. And we are all better for it. Who else would have made us a priority? Who else would have taken the time to think about more than just ending the fight?

"This planet needed *you* to be the person who fought for it, otherwise... who knows what we would have had. I look at Amy and I see the future. That future is only going to be one worth living in because of you. Never forget that."

Moss took in the words. He did not think of himself in those terms but hearing them he hoped they were true. They would clean the water and then they would finish what they started. Moss had just spent so much time trying to encourage others and it was a kindness to get some himself.

"You are a good man, Gil," Moss said, struggling to find the right words.

"You are, too, Moss," Gil said. "*All* the life of this world owes you a debt of gratitude."

Moss smiled, feeling full. "Tell that kiddo of yours that she is really quite something."

Gil smiled but rolled his eyes and laughed. "Oh, she already knows. But I'll pass along the message."

"Please do," Moss said. "See you soon."

"See you soon," Gil said with a smile and Moss turned to board the ship. As he got on, he saw his friends holding up the warden armor they were about to put on.

He turned to Judy and said, "This must be weird for you?"

"I haven't actually worn armor since basic," Judy said. "You have to remember that I was a mechanic for the company, so my uniform was just coveralls with the logo stitched on."

"Maybe that's what we've been missing," Gibbs said.

"What's that?" Issy asked.

"Uniforms," Gibbs said. "We're always stealing other people's or having to wear borrowed Dermidoses, but maybe we should have been in our own uniforms this whole time."

Judy laughed. "I would love to see all of you guys dressed like Ynna."

"Oh, shit, we all know I would look *great* in that shredded skirt," Gibbs announced, puffing himself up as he pointed toward Ynna's outfit.

Ynna rolled her eyes. "Yeah, you would look hot, but I don't want anyone borrowing my look."

"Actually," Issy interjected, "I saw a couple of people with your exact look when we met with the other teams. I think your look is trending a bit."

Despite what she had just claimed, Ynna immediately brightened and asked, "Really?"

"Yeah," Issy affirmed.

Moss nodded. "Me too, actually."

"That's so cool!" Ynna exclaimed. Moss loved how excited she was as she watched the rest of them get into their borrowed Carcer outfits. "I'm really going to miss this."

Issy chuckled. "I would trade with you in a heartbeat."

The comment made Moss's heart race, thinking about the implication.

"Oh, no you wouldn't," Ynna said. "You love this action-movie shit as much as I do. It's the boys who would happily sit it out."

Gibbs chuckled. "One hundred percent."

"Not that you guys could handle pregnancy," Ynna mocked.

"Yeah," Gibbs said as he pulled on the black pants and began affixing the armor plates. "I have no interest in peeing myself when I sneeze."

Ynna looked horrified. "Is that a thing?"

Issy nodded. "You've never had pregnant friends?"

"Not really," Ynna admitted.

Issy laughed. "Oh, girl, you are in for a world of hurt."

"Ugh," she groaned, pulling her pink hair back into a ponytail. "I take it back. Gibbs, you can be the pregnant one and I'll go shoot everyone."

"No takesies backsies!" Gibbs said and they smiled at one another in that way that made Moss's heart happy.

Patchwork had finished putting on the armor and sat down next Moss. "This is hella weird."

"You forget about it pretty quick," Moss told him.

"I doubt that," Patchwork said. "Just like the forces of oppression will never feel okay. It isn't something you forget."

"Fair point," Moss admitted. "Things with you and Tak good?"

"Yeah," Patchwork said and a little smile crossed his lips. "They're good."

"And you're ready for this?" Moss asked, gesturing around the ship.

Patchwork lit a cigarette and looked around. "You know I don't love coming on these missions. Y'all seem to get off on 'somehow not getting killed' but not me. I like just regular 'not getting killed,' from the safety of my chair back at the safe house."

"I know, trust me," Moss said. "I wouldn't make you come if I didn't have to. Plus, you know…"

"Yeah," Patchwork said with a chuckle, "my mom scares the shit out of me too."

"She's the only person who could make Sandra back down," Moss observed, feeling the familiar pang of guilt he did every time he brought up his grandmother. The conversation with his father had quieted the program but hadn't done anything to alleviate how he felt. He could ignore it, justify it and push it to the side, but he would always know what he had done and have to live with it. He still believed he had to do it but it was fucked up and he knew it.

"My mom could make *anyone* back down," Patchwork laughed. "One of the reasons I didn't have a lot of friends growing up was that no one wanted to come to my place."

"Right," Ynna chuckled from across the ship. "*That's what it was…*"

Patchwork looked sincerely wounded by the comment but before Moss could offer some consolation, Issy said, "I'm sure none of us were particularly cool as kids."

Heads nodded as everyone finished pulling on their armor. "I was," Judy said and all heads turned. "You're not getting some whole story, here, but suffice to say, I was the cool kid."

"Judy," Ynna said, "I don't think there's a single person on the ship who doesn't believe that."

Judy laughed and then, seeing everyone was serious, laughed again. "Guess I thought it would take more convincing."

The drudge pilot let them know they were nearing their destination. Moss turned to Ynna.

"We didn't have anybody who could've just stepped in?"

Looking at the drudge, she said, "Well, we either could have taught someone to fly this thing or found someone to teach them. Neither option seemed particularly pleasant or safe, given everything, so a machine seemed like the easiest answer."

"Machines can be hacked," Moss said ominously.

Ynna looked annoyed. "You can be hacked!" she snapped. "And, anyway, I don't see you learning how to fly a fucking spaceship."

Moss held up his hands defensively. "You're right, sorry I said anything."

"It could be a long nine months," Gibbs joked.

"Say something like that again and you'll last nine more seconds," Ynna said and Moss and Gibbs fell silent.

The ship banked and started its descent. They had given coordinates near, but not too near, the pump station. The drone footage they had gathered indicated that ThutoCo had overrun the place with its hired agents and remaining Zetas. They were not going to give this location up without a fight and Moss knew it.

The side door slid open and Moss saw the wardens waiting for them. Judy, Ynna, Gibbs and Issy all hopped out. Before making her way over to join the others, Issy turned back and looked right at Patchwork. "You keep him alive, okay?"

Patchwork smiled and nodded. "I'll do my best."

"Do better than your best," Issy said and turned to Moss. "And you, I love you."

"You better," he said and winked. Issy rolled her eyes as the ship began to lift again. Moss stood and picked up the dronepack. He turned to Patchwork and said, "Ready?"

"Not really," Patch admitted, but he stood and turned as Moss helped affix the thing to his back. He then did the same for Moss, and they both stepped over to the open door.

Clutching the handrail and gazing down at the water treatment plant, Patchwork muttered under his breath, "Got me jumping out of the dropship into enemy territory…" followed by a bunch of audible expletives.

Moss wasn't particularly keen on the view either. The wind whipping his face as they stood so high above the earth in the middle of the night did not make him want to leap. He would prefer to just strap himself back in. But if any of this was going to work, they needed to do this.

His face must have displayed his trepidation, because Patchwork turned and said, "There has to be some other way."

Moss shook his head and pulled on his helmet, handing the other one to Patchwork. "There isn't," Moss said as Patch put his helmet on too., "Sorry, Patch."

His hand moved to Patchwork's back and Moss felt the familiar sensation of pushing somebody from a great height. The image of Sandra falling flooded his mind as Patch let go of the handrail and began plummeting toward the earth. Unlike his grandmother, Patchwork's dronepack fired to life and guided him gently toward the preprogrammed destination.

Moss let himself fall, feeling how she must have felt as the weight of his body carried him careening towards the ground. He felt sick to his stomach before the dronepack kicked in, adjusting his body and carrying him downward.

The display in his helmet began to scan the environment for enemies, marking heat signatures all around the plant. There were a lot of them. As they were marked, The Kids got into position. Judy and Patchwork had been working for a long time on a fleet of microdrones that could be deployed at the same time and take simultaneous action.

As he was falling, Patchwork was also marking any targets that he saw.

The plant itself was comprised of several large buildings beside large circular pools with metal bridges. Lights flashed on top of the structures and agents were posted everywhere. They would know to be on the lookout and everything would have to go flawlessly for this to work.

"You think we got them all?" Moss asked.

The earpiece in his helmet crackled and Patchwork said, "Sure hope so."

"You can do the honors."

"Would have been pretty fucked for you not to let me." Patchwork noted all the small drones and went to work at once. As Moss and Patchwork neared the roof of a building, dozens of small weapons fired at once. Little projectile darts hit the gaps in the armor before microscopic tendrils sought out veins and injected the neurotoxin.

Agents began to fall across the complex and, as expected, the deaths triggered alarms. Lights began to flash and alarms blared and Moss could see in the distance the wardens making their way toward the fence line.

More agents that hadn't been marked poured from the buildings and began firing immediately. Wardens rushed forward, firing back, and bodies began to fall on both sides. As the war raged, Moss and Patchwork landed on the roof of the main building. Patchwork turned to Moss.

"How much I hated that fall nearly ruined how cool it was to see The Kids in action."

"I agree… nearly…" Moss said with a smirk. "Now let's go save the city."

CHAPTER 9

M oss sipped his coffee, feeling like his brain had returned a bit after sleeping. It had not been restful at first. Issy had snored like a chainsaw and his mind had raced thinking of everything that had happened; but once he had fallen asleep, it had been a sleep like death. The sun was already threatening to set by the time he awakened, and even Issy was out of bed.

Patchwork Using his cybernetic leg, Moss kicked the lock off the roof access door which was little more than a swinging piece of metal with a handle. The place was not constructed to withstand an invasion or be the focal point of a battle; it was simply an industrial water station. The agents had taken it over but they had still been taken unawares.

The sounds of the skirmish below drowned out the scraping noises made by Moss and Patch as they climbed into the hatch and down the ladder. At the bottom, it was little more than cement walls with some industrial supplies for roof repairs. There was also a little chair in the corner with a box of tissues and hand moisturizer.

"That's grim," Patchwork said as he looked at the metal folding chair with ripped padding.

Moss nodded and turned his head to the thick, reinforced door. It hadn't been constructed for security reasons but for sound dampening. Looking back at the chair, Moss realized this was what passed for a break room. He looked at Patchwork and held a finger to the front of the helmet. Patch nodded and Moss opened the door.

The deafening roar hit them first. It sounded like a waterfall. The rushing water was oppressive to the point that it vibrated the ground underfoot. The building was a labyrinth of massive pipes. A metal footbridge led outward and there were stairs going down.

Under them were more pipes and massive cisterns. Pools for treating water and vats of chemicals filled the spaces between and the air was damp and misty, fogging their visors instantly. Moss could see the agents set on sentry around the building. All were on high alert, their bodies poised and waiting. As planned, they were all looking toward the door, waiting for invaders.

Moss couldn't help but wonder what it was like for them — some private security company picked up by ThutoCo when Carcer was forced from the city. These people, who had probably guarded small businesses and apartment buildings, were now asked to stand against righteous crusaders. He wondered if they just did it for the money or if they were happy to finally have an excuse to fight and kill. Perhaps they had always wanted to hurt others but never had an excuse.

He couldn't help going down the rabbit hole in his mind as he moved up the catwalk. They moved quickly, because anyone who looked up would be able to see them. There was no visual barrier, just a metal handrail nearly rusted through.

An agent stood guard on the catwalk but was leaning on the rail, looking down onto his allies. The overwhelming sound of water covered their approach and Moss was able to put his Kingfisher right into a gap in the armor, pulling the trigger and easing the guard onto the gangway. The armor was advanced and Moss wished that he had killed the guy who created it when he recently had the chance.

There were few gaps in the plates and everything was connected electronically, so the armor moved fluidly with the wearer. There were people inside, but the armor almost made them look like military drudges rather than humans. The face plates had digital display screens which flashed shapes. Moss had come to understand that the agents were able to use them to communicate with one another.

Moss and Patchwork crept forward. Patch had pulled his weapon but Moss knew the young man did not want to use it. His mother, Jo, had been a brilliant soldier in the war versus the South a generation earlier but Patchwork was a gentler soul. He had enthusiastically joined missions but had been injured and didn't seem to have the 'fight' that so many of the rest of the crew had. Even Gibbs had discovered a hidden fire within that made him a skilled fighter in the right circumstances, but Patchwork always seemed more content to hang back and stay safe. And with breakers, that tended to be all that was necessary.

They kept moving, Moss's eyes flashing downward constantly, making sure that none of the agents caught sight of them. They were severely outnumbered and this mission would be successful only if they kept quiet and their friends kept up the distraction.

They neared a small security office at the end of the catwalk and Moss raised his weapon. Patchwork did the same, but Moss knew that it was up to him.

Opening the door slowly, he peeked in to see a lone guard in the room pressing her hand to the side of her helmet and hissing loudly, "No, I don't know when I'm going to get off today... it's a special assignment... no, no, listen to me... No, I understand that, but I can either earn money or be home with the kids, I can't be in two places at once…"

Moss moved in close, feeling a bit guilty as he found a gap in the armor and pulled the trigger once more. Like with the other guard, Moss eased her to the ground slowly.

"Dude," Patchwork said sadly. "Sucks that she won't be home soon to help with the kids."

"No," Moss sighed quietly, "what sucks is marrying a partner that demands you to both make the money *and* watch the kids while they do squat."

Patchwork nodded in agreement and said, "The control room is downstairs and across the floor from here. I'm sure you've noticed that there are a lot of people between us and there."

"I know. And you're doing a great job. Just stay quiet and stay behind me, and we'll reach the control room in no time."

"All good, man," Patch said, and Moss could hear the smile. "A lot of people are dying and this is going to do a lot of good."

Moss nodded, happy to hear that Patch was feeling confident and inspired even though they were infiltrating a position and surrounded by people who would kill them as soon as look at them. Staying low, they moved toward the little window and peered out to get a better look at the positions of their enemies.

Thankfully, they weren't patrolling but staying still and now that the two had a moment, they began tagging the targets.

"There will be some we can't see," Moss reminded Patchwork, who nodded in understanding.

"The fu—" a voice said. but before it could even finish the word, Moss had fired three bolts in quick succession. Two sizzled against the thick, densely plated armor, but one found a groove. They agent crumpled to the ground and Moss raced across the room to the far door through which he had stepped. Behind the agent was a metal staircase and his body was tilting in that direction.

Moss grabbed the collar of the man's armor just before he tipped down the stairs. But the man was heavy in the massive armor and began to drag Moss forward, but in a moment, he felt arms around his waist and Patchwork pulled the two of them back into the security office. They all fell into a pile and Moss had the wind knocked out of him, but fortunately they had not alerted the others to their presence.

As Moss pushed the man off him and onto the sheet metal floor, Patchwork said, "I guess that's why we want to be aware of the ones we can't see, eh?"

Moss chuckled as he helped his friend up off the ground. "Exactly."

"You have become one hell of a shot," Patchwork observed.

"Practice," Moss said with a shrug.

"Yeah, the kind of practice that can get you killed..." Patchwork noted.

"Got that right," Moss said.

He gestured toward the door through which the agent had just appeared. Moss headed for the door with Patch behind him and peeked out, checking for more surprises before descending the metal staircase. They had to move slowly because their boots on the thin metal rattled and clanged. The whole thing bounced and swayed and felt as if it was going to collapse at any moment.

Reaching the bottom, they ducked behind a forklift beside pallets of barrels. Down here, the sound of water and smell of chemicals were even worse and Moss had to rely entirely on his vision. The marked targets were highlighted and he could still see them through the walls, barrels and machinery.

Knowing that there were many agents they had not marked and seeing the sheer numbers of the ones they had, Moss had to take a calming breath before abandoning his temporary cover.

Using the helmet's digital display integrated with his own cybernetic eyes, Patchwork marked the door they were trying to reach. Moss gave him a quick thumbs up and they both began to slink forward, keeping one eye on the targets they had and the other on the ones they didn't. They stayed low, moved slowly and kept near the machinery. Ducking under a curved pipe, they ended up beside a pump with another agent between them and their destination.

He was facing away, toward the heavy doors at the front of the building where most of their crew was making its assault. Moss inched forward, getting as close as he could before making his move. He glanced around quickly to be sure that nobody else was in the vicinity and then darted like a snake, wrapping an elbow around the man's neck while simultaneously shooting him in the gap between plates.

– Moss dragged him back as the bolt did its work and laid the body beside the massive metal cube of dripping rust, valve control wheels and pressure indicators. He hated to leave the body out in the open like this, but there was no easy place to hide it and moving a body was hard enough without the heavy mechanized armor. So, he stepped over the body and peered around the side of the machine, glancing back and forth to make sure the coast was clear.

He waved Patchwork up but as Patch moved around the body, it spasmed and its arm moved, hitting Patchwork in the shin. He screamed and the sound cut through the other noise. Both men immediately pressed their backs against the machinery and waited, Moss feeling his heart in his throat. He turned his helmet toward one of the agents they had tagged and could see him pressing his hands to the sides of his helmet.

Someone had been alerted and was radioing the others. Moss tried to calculate which was worse, staying or going. His heart pounded against his chest as he tried to decide quickly and he could see that Patchwork's hands were shaking violently. Moss didn't think it was so much from the mortal peril they were in than the fact that Patchwork blamed himself for what was happening.

The decision was made for him as another agent could be heard approaching their position from between the pipes. Moss and Patchwork raced to a spot just across the pathway. Their backs had hit their new spots just before the agent came running up, weapon pointed at their felled compatriot.

Wasting no time, Moss popped out and repeated his attack technique, wrapping his arm around and pressing the weapon. Just then, out of the corner of his eye, he saw a second agent converge from the other side. The agent skidded to a stop as he saw Moss and the two bodies. There was a brief moment of paralysis as the agent seemed too shocked to act. But a moment later, he raised his weapon right at Moss.

Patchwork moved like a blur and copied Moss's method. Six shots sizzled against the armor before he managed to find the gap and the man began to thrash. As Moss eased his victims to the ground, Patchwork and his fell backward against the giant pipe, their armor clinging dully against the thick metal. As Patchwork rolled his agent onto the floor, Moss kept his weapon primed, pointing back and forth between the two sides.

No one else was approaching and the agents displayed through their helmets didn't appear to be leaving their posts. Moss let out a long sigh of relief but could see his own hand shaking with nerves. Turning back to Patchwork, he nodded and gave another thumbs up before turning to leave this location.

As he was about to make his way through the gap, he felt a hand on his shoulder. He turned quickly, his gun pointed right at Patchwork who whispered, "I'm so sorry."

This wasn't the time or the place for an apology, but Moss knew how Patchwork felt and couldn't begrudge his instinct. It was one that he shared, himself. Even in the heat of pitch battle, he would sometimes feel an emotion that felt utterly out of place.

"It's all good," Moss told him and reached out to pat him reassuringly on the shoulder with a closed fist. Patchwork nodded and Moss wished he could see his friend's face, but he hoped he was relieved. He didn't need Patch getting into his own head and making any foolish mistakes.

They quickly moved to the next hiding spot and then the next. Moss knocked out another two agents and left them where they fell. They were racking up a lot of bodies and Moss was starting to get very nervous that a patrol would stumble upon one of them. His plan had been to take down as few as they could but they had all been positioned in his way.

Soon, they were nearing the control room. The bright yellow door displayed in the helmet was just on the other side of a huge open vat and the two men moved quickly, keeping their shoulders near but not against the metal vessel. There were no more agents nearby displayed in the helmet and they darted across the little path to the door. Moss tried the handle and realized it was locked. Patchwork approached and got to work. He knelt by the computer array beside the door as Moss guarded his back. They were exposed, too exposed for Moss's taste. They had no other choice, but the moment was terrifying.

Moss didn't even hear the click of the door but just saw Patchwork pushing it open. He turned, ready for the battle to commence, but as they stepped in he was utterly surprised by what he saw.

CHAPTER 12

The room was empty of people. Moss kept pointing his weapon around in disbelief, waiting for someone to appear but it didn't happen.

Looking more closely, he realized it wouldn't have even been possible. The room was little more than rows of computer monitors against the left and right walls with a small conference table bisecting them. Closing the door behind them, Patchwork pulled his helmet off.

"How do these guys wear these all day?" he asked. "After five minutes the whole place just smelled like sweat and burp breath."

Pulling his own helmet off, Moss said, "It's true. It's just all coffee breath all the time in there for me… I don't get it, though."

"Get what?" Patchwork asked as he stepped over to one of the control consoles.

"There should be someone in here. Why wouldn't they station someone in the control room?"

"Don't know, don't care," Patch said with a shrug and one of his eyes went black. The computer he stood in front of crackled and the screen began to display streams of code.

It didn't feel right. Moss was more on edge because the place was deserted than he would've been if he had to shoot three people. Spotting a little door, he walked over to the restroom and raised his Kingfisher as he put his left hand on the handle. He swung the door open quickly with weapon at the ready, but no one was there.

He turned back into the control room and stared at the monitors. One camera positioned on an elevated tower pointed at the heart of the battle. Most of the agents had positioned themselves behind cover and were well entrenched. Moss's crew had put up small shield walls but were exposed on the approaching road and unable to move forward. Squinting into the monitor, it appeared that neither side had sustained any casualties and were mostly just trading pot shots.

Moss was pleased with that. He would rather not see dead agents as long as they had not lost anyone either. He couldn't shake the feeling that he had missed something, and he turned to scan the room again but still saw nothing out of the ordinary.

He strode over to a small locker against the wall and opened it. There was nothing inside but some clothes and old magazines. The space wasn't even big enough to fit a person. Despite himself, he just had to accept that these agents were not all that good at their jobs.

"Any reason not to do this thing?" Patch work asked.

Moss shrugged. "Do it."

Suddenly, the building began to shake and vibrate. It felt like one of the famous B.A. City earthquakes but it was sustained in a way the natural disasters were not. As the roof began to open and the garage doors clattered up, Moss watched on the monitors as the agents began looking around in terror. He saw them wave and call out to one another, flash symbols on their faceplates and press their hands to their heads as they tried to communicate amid the confusion.

Many of the agents began retreating into the building, preparing for whatever was coming. As they turned to run, they were taken out one by one by Gibbs, obviously well-hidden in an elevated position on the far side. The wardens who had been hiding along the road rushed up and began moving toward the facility. Issy and Judy fell in with them, rushing toward the chain-link fence slowly rattling aside.

They all opened fire at once and the screen flashed and flared. The agents returned fire from their superior positions behind cover and many of the wardens fell as they stormed in. The moment the wardens cleared the gate, Issy chucked a grenade towards some entrenched agents. The camera shook and went white for a moment before revealing the wardens continuing their push. Watching it on the screen, Moss couldn't help but feel bad for most everyone involved. Moss and his friends had a purpose, a reason for being here and doing what they were doing but both the wardens and agents were people who were doing this for no other reason than a paycheck. They were shooting and killing one another because their bosses told them to. It was a grim reminder of what the companies had done- normalizing corporate warfare devoid of just purpose.

Moss could hear shouting outside and realized that the agents were finally storming his position as they were falling back. He checked the charge on his Kingfisher and pressed his shoulder against the door frame before cracking the door open a bit. He didn't see anyone coming but some of the tagged targets were converging on his position. As soon as one rounded the corner, he popped off a couple of shots before realizing he had made a mistake. His Kingfisher was good, but against these well armored soldiers he needed something with a little bit more power.

Closing the door behind him, he rushed over to the nearest body and picked up the high-powered rifle off the ground beside it. Moss poked his head out from beside the cover and leveled a new weapon at one of the approaching agents. Squeezing the trigger, he felt the kick on his shoulder as the thing blasted. The opposing agent was shredded on the left side from shoulder to head, bits of metal, electronics, flesh and bone spraying out. What was left of the body was blasted to the ground and Moss felt the weapon reload itself. It was a terrifyingly powerful piece of weaponry and Moss realized what the wardens and his friends were up against, before it occurred to him that he was as well.

Two more agents came rushing towards him and Moss took another shot, propelling one backward. The remaining one blasted a shot toward Moss before ducking behind cover. The agent's shot exploded over Moss's head, shredding one of the pipes and sending water gushing out. The cascade hit Moss's shoulder, the force knocking him to the ground. The agent peeking out from behind his hiding spot took this as an opportunity to close in on Moss, who was trying to force himself to his feet in the torrent.

The agent took another shot and Moss rolled out of the way just in time as water and bits of cement burst next to his shoulder. Moss fired back wildly, rupturing another pipe and sending the agents ducking for cover once more. Staggering to his feet, Moss raised his weapon and shot at the machinery the man had ducked behind before remembering that he needed it to function. The metal casing was shredded but the machine continued to pump away.

The agent popped out and took a shot, rocketing back the barrel that Moss had put between himself and his opponent. Moss had to jump out of the way and was starting to get annoyed. This agent was taking too long to go down and as he was having that thought, another rounded the corner. From his position in the pool on the ground, he got a clean chest shot, ripping the man's armor completely apart and sending his body flying back.

Fear and rage motivating him, Moss leapt to his feet and looked around the corner to see the agent doing the same thing. Quickly, he inched his body a little bit further out and instantly back behind cover. In that time, the agent took the shot that Moss had expected and as soon as it went off, Moss rounded the corner and charged the agent.

The agent's body language registered his shock as he fell backward before Moss advanced and fired a shot at such close range that it splattered the agent against the floor. Moss sloshed through the reddening water back to the door to ensure that Patchwork was still safe.

"How you holding up?" Moss asked.

Patchwork gave a thumbs up. "Doing great over here, but I have to upload all these programs and ensure they're installed correctly or we will end up polluting the water by adding too much of the cure. It's a super delicate balance, you know?"

Moss nodded and moved back out to keep his friend safe. Another agent charged him, but as Moss raised his weapon the man fell forward, splashing into the pooling water as a warden appeared.

Judy was hot on the warden's heels and Moss called out, "Continue to secure the area, there are more behind."

Moss fell in beside them and they began to clear out the building.

"Thanks for opening the door," Judy said with a smile.

"These agents make the ThutoCo Zetas look like Knights of the Round Table," Moss joked.

Judy shrugged as they rounded the corner and devastated another agent with a blast from their shotgun. Stepping over to the fallen agent, Judy picked their powerful rifle up into their own hand and examined it. "Yeah, but they got good toys."

Thinking about the destructive shots he had taken with the agent's weapons, Moss smirked and said, "That they do."

Moss and Judy had to duck as a piece of wall exploded behind them, sending chunks flying around them. The warden by their side aimed and took two precision shots, sending bullets cleanly into the gaps of the agent's armor.

"Shouldn't be joking around in the heat of battle," the warden scolded before disappearing between two pipes.

Moss rolled his eyes, but as he turned to Judy, he saw distress in their eyes.

"What's the big deal?"

They shook their head and smiled weakly. "I was Carcer for a long time and those kinds of comments from somebody who would have been my superior still land."

"I get that," Moss nodded. "The human mind is a helluva thing."

"That it is," Judy said with a smile

"Guys," Issy called from the far side of the corridor and they both turned to her. As she waved them over, they could hear the honks of trucks and see the lights of the descending dropship. Craning his head upward, Moss saw the industrial sized container of antidote.

He began clattering his way up the metal ladder on the side of the cistern. He ran out into the middle of the long walkway which connected the two sides. In the center was a large metal frame into which the containers engineered at the Conservation would fit perfectly. Kneeling, Moss reached to unscrew the valve cap, but discovered that years of disuse in a damp room had made it nearly inoperable.

He ran back to where he had seen a large wrench sitting beside the ladder. He grabbed it and hurried back, clanging it down and pointing the teeth upward to grab the wheel. Torquing it hard, he felt it give and the rest crumbled, allowing the wheel to move. Moss was sweating and could hear more gunshots in the distance. It was a strange thing to do this work while there was still a pitched battle going on around him. But it needed to be done and needed to be done now.

The antidote tank kept lowering toward him as trucks pulled around with more and wardens hopped into the driver's seats of the specially modified forklifts. The tank was strapped with come-alongs chained to a hook at the bottom of the dropship, and the tank itself had a tapered end leading to a valved release. As it moved closer, Moss reached up to guide the tank slowly toward the hole at the bottom of the walkway. The long, bracing I-beams groaned as the metal slid into place.

Moss continued to help steer it until the tip found the opening, the bottom of the vat pointing directly into the top of the water. Now came the tricky part. Moss began to slowly turn the tank, watching to ensure that the corresponding threaded grooves found one another. Carl had stressed the importance of screwing in the vat. Timed release of the proper amount was paramount, and if the tank came loose and added either not enough or too much, all of this would have been for naught.

He felt the tank catch and had to spin it backward and start again. More shots rang out but they were becoming fewer as the wardens took out the last of the agents. As Moss turned the massive thing again, he breathed a bit easier. With this in place and with the agents dealt with, ThutoCo's strength was being chipped away. They had made their big move and though so many lives had been lost, the situation was being remedied.

It was a remarkable thing and without all these hired agents, ThutoCo had very little defense against them now.

They could take the fight to Arthur Smith directly.

Moss felt the click as the tank moved perfectly into place and he hurried to remove the straps so the dropship could pull away. Chained as it was, the whole operation was vulnerable and even one remaining agent could disrupt everything. Releasing the clamp, Moss waved up to the ship as the straps came loose and pulled away. Now, with the tank in place, Moss ran to the control room.

"I don't remember adding 'doing math' to my resume when I joined you guys," Patch said as Moss entered the room.

"And what's worse is that we don't even pay you for this."

"Yeah, this life of a rebel thing is a total fucking scam." Patch laughed. "We're getting close. Most of the vats are in place and I've done all the requisite calculations."

"You really are quite something," Moss said.

"I expect a plaque at the very least."

"And here I was thinking that a trophy would do," Moss offered with a wry smile. He glanced around the room again, just to be sure, and it was still empty.

"Last ones in place... and here we go," Patchwork said.

Moss watched as the screens began to display liquid ratios and waterflow charts. Moss was terrified of the reports they would get from the mayor's office. All those people dead, but he could take solace in the fact that they had stopped it, stemmed the blood flow. It wasn't perfect but it was something.

He heard a clatter behind him, then another sound and turned with his weapon raised. A panel had fallen off a computer bank on the far wall, exposing an agent who had been hiding there, likely hoping to simply survive. Moss saw the smoking weapon in the agent's hand and felt himself pull the trigger. Gore sprayed all over the secret compartment and Moss looked down to see how badly he had been shot.

But there was nothing. Out of the corner of his ear, he heard Patchwork say, "Shit."

CHAPTER 11

The dropship raced across the city at a nauseating speed. The last time Patchwork had been hurt, his mother had said that if anything ever happened to him again, he was to be brought straight to her. The force of the thrusters blew out the glass on one of the high-rise buildings as they rocketed passed.

"I'm not hurt that bad," Patchwork said, gripping his side.

"I know," Moss told him, patting him on the chest

He wasn't seriously injured but the shot had gone through part of the flesh on his side. Moss had treated him quickly with healing spray but he needed proper medical attention. The drugs left him feeling no pain, but Patchwork would be out of commission for a while.

"Judy just let me know the water has been purified," Gibbs said as he approached from the back. "We did it."

Moss felt relief wash over him. A lot of people had died but they had stemmed the bleeding. "Preliminary numbers?"

"None yet, but it would have been a lot worse if not for us," Gibbs said, pride pervading his words.

"Hear that?" Moss asked, looking back to Patchwork.

The kid smiled weakly. "Saved the world again?"

"Almost," Moss smiled. "We certainly helped a lot of people."

"That's nice," Patchwork said, his eyes distant and vacant. Even though he knew Patchwork would be okay, Moss hated to see his friend like this. He was such a sweet soul and, in his own way, so delicate. It broke Moss's heart to know he was hurting.

The thrusters slowed and the ship began to descend. Moss stood and readied himself beside the door. Gibbs came around and stood ready on the other side of the board on which Patchwork lay.

They could feel the ship settle as the landing feet hit the cement and the door began to hiss open. The door had only lowered a third of the way before Jo was inside and kneeling beside her son.

"Oh baby, look what they've done to you. I love you, mommy's here," she soothed, running her hand along his face. His eyes brightened then, and he smiled.

It was as heartwarming as it was heartbreaking. It made Moss long for his own family, wish his parents hadn't been killed and wish his grandmother hadn't needed to be. His heart ached, but Jo turned fierce eyes on him and snapped, "Come on!"

The door was now open enough so they could lift the gurney and carry Patchwork out. Two people in Crassun Emergency Services uniforms rushed over to meet them and gestured in the direction of an unmarked van. The van's rear doors were open and within was state-of-the-art emergency equipment. Moss, Gibbs and Jo carried Patchwork over to the vehicle and loaded him in with the two off-duty emergency response professionals.

Moss found it amusing that two people who worked for the ubiquitous aid company also had side gigs doing the same thing. He also wondered how much Jo was paying to have these people on standby but was coming to understand what parents would do for their children.

Moss and Gibbs had already pulled off Patch's armor and stripped him to the waist, so the responders got to work on the wound immediately. The medics began shoving the three of them out of the van saying, "He'll be fine but you need to give us space. Jo, will you park on the roof of the Talisman."

Jo nodded as she hopped out and swung the doors closed behind her, pounding twice with her fist and watching as the van began hovering away. to Moss as he opened his mouth to apologize but then saw white. She had hit him faster than any person ever had and harder than the impact of a bullet hitting armor. Blinking, he realized that he was gasping for air and on the ground. His head throbbed and pain radiated out of his eye.

Jo was a slender older woman, but as powerful a human being Moss had ever met and she had just proven it.

"I told Burn I didn't want you to take him, and I told Sandra I didn't want you to take him, but none of y'all listened to me and now look how my boy is! You got him gutshot but good and you ain't never gonna take him again," she screamed down at him, backlit by the streetlamp.

"I will never take him again," Moss rasped.

"Sure as shit you won't," Jo affirmed and reached out a hand. Moss grabbed it and she helped him to his feet. "Come on, let's get you boys a drink."

More than a drink, Moss wanted ice for his eye. He still couldn't believe how easily she had dropped him. He had known her to be a veteran of the wars, but he had thought of himself as pretty tough too. That punch made him feel like he was just playing at hero.

Gibbs patted Moss on the back and the two followed Jo down the street to her bar, the Talisman Saloon. It didn't take long to reach the place and Moss remembered that first time, when Burn had walked him this very way. It felt like another world to Moss, for he had been so different. He had been like a new baby, unaccustomed to this world; and now he needed a stiff drink after another gun battle.

They stepped into the bar and saw the usual barfly regulars and a naked waiter who was easily the best looking and most fit man Moss had ever seen. He couldn't help but stare as they sat at the bar and Jo walked around to grab a whiskey bottle. She plunked three large shot glasses on the counter and started pouring.

"I expected this shit from the old folks, but I never expected it of you," she said, scorn evident in her words. She took a gulp of her drink and looked the two of them over. Moss and Gibbs did their shots too and she continued. "See, this is why children need to stay close to their parents and why parents need to stay alive for their children. Too many generations of lost parents have made too many lost children. You all need to take a long hard look in the mirror."

"Feel like my life has become nothing but a long hard look in the mirror," Moss said, holding his glass up for a refill.

"You're right," Gibbs said.

"No kidding I'm right," Jo said, clinking her glass against Gibbs's. "You can't live this long and not know a thing or two. Shit, people who don't know a thing or two *don't* live this long."

"I have no idea how the two of us have survived," Moss admitted, thinking of all the times he had been shot, blown up or beaten. By all rights, he should have been killed countless times. He had just been some idiot kid when he left the burbs and had no training or idea of what he was doing. He should have died countless times over, yet here he was.

"Don't…" Gibbs began but trailed off a moment before continuing, "Don't you want to go be with Patchwork?"

Jo sighed and frowned. "No," she said. "*Willis* will be okay and I will just get in the way of the docs. The last thing they need is some worried mother pissing in their ear and questioning their work. If I've learned anything about battlefield medicine, it's that folks like me only make things worse."

Gibbs nodded and Moss said, "Sorry we got him shot."

"I'm sorry you got him shot, too," Jo snapped before sucking in a deep breath and letting it out slowly. "You guys are just kids, like we were. Burn, your grandmother and me. We didn't know what the fuck we were doing either."

Her eyes were distant, locked into some memory. "They handed us guns and pushed us toward other kids with guns. One fucked-up mess. Then the cycle continued. Burn and Sandra… they didn't train you… not properly, anyway. They just did the same thing with you that the companies did to us. It all comes back around."

Moss and Gibbs didn't speak. They were both swimming in their own deep oceans of thoughts.

"I know you're trying your best. Just hard to give a fuck how hard y'all are trying when my boy is shot."

"I know," Moss said, and he did. He had always hated having to put Patchwork in harm's way, and now the decision had come home to roost.

Turning to Gibbs, he saw that his friend had gone somewhere else entirely.

"She should have helped you more, though. I know she tried," Jo added.

"She did," Moss said, feelings of guilt and disgust rising. He took another gulp, felt the alcohol burn through him and his head began to swim. He had just helped save the people of the city and all he felt was a deep self-loathing for all he had done.

"She loved you, boy, did she love you," Jo said quietly.

The knife in his heart twisted and he felt like he might vomit. Sweat began to build on his brow. "In her own way," he croaked, unsure what to say.

Jo snorted a laugh. "In her own way…"

Moss didn't want to think about how she had loved him.

"Family is all we have," Moss said. "When everything else falls away, it's the people we love that matter."

"Amen," Jo said, raising a glass. "Even if that family ain't blood."

"Especially then," Moss said, clapping Gibbs on the back. Gibbs looked up like he had been awakened from a trance.

"Cheers," he said and took his shot.

Gibbs turned to look at Moss with red, terrified eyes. Jo opened her mouth to speak but the door burst open and Tak came running in, his face streaked with tears. Jo darted out from around the counter and rushed over to embrace him.

"He's going to be fine," she assured the young man. He nodded but didn't say anything for a long moment.

"Where is he?" he asked, and Moss remembered how he had felt when Issy had been recently hospitalized.

"He's being treated. Come on, we'll wait together," Jo said, wrapping an arm over the young man's shoulder and grabbing the bottle off of the counter.

Tak turned to Moss. "There are other crews you know," he snarled. "It doesn't always have to be a one-man show."

"I'm sorry," Moss stammered. "We knew you guys were busy with other things."

"Not too busy for this," Tak said, his voice breaking.

It was hard to hear. Tak had always been so reverential of Moss and now he was just another leader angry that he didn't get to help.

"You're right," Moss said. "It won't happen again."

"Better not," Tak said as Jo pushed him towards one of the little tables.

"I know he's just coming from a place of hurt but, like, I don't feel bad enough already..." Moss groused.

"Oh, boo fucking hoo," Gibbs snapped, and Moss couldn't believe it.

"What's up your ass?" Moss asked, trying not to be annoyed and failing.

Gibbs shook his head, clearly trying to decide what to say next. He never seemed to be a loss for words but something was obviously eating him. Moss softened.

"What's going on, man?"

"It's this, all of this," Gibbs said.

"What about it?"

"Something has changed within me, something is not the same," Gibbs singsonged with a weak little smile.

He always reverted to quotes when he was hurting, but Moss didn't get the reference. He felt like he understood them less and less as his old life became an increasingly distant memory. Moss didn't speak, he just waited for his friend to continue.

"Ever since I learned... learned about the baby, I don't know... my heart's just not in this."

That was the last thing that Moss wanted to hear. Worse was that he understood why his friend felt this way.

"This was never your fight," Moss said. "You brought me to the city to keep your friend safe and got shot for your

113

troubles. You got swept up in something and found reasons to stay involved but you were never in this for yourself."

Gibbs looked at him in surprise and cracked a small smile. "I expected this to be more of a revelatory moment."

Moss laughed. "I know how you like your big reveals. Sorry to disappoint."

"You know I'll stick by your side to the end," Gibbs told him.

"I know," Moss said, feeling another wave of emotion crash over him. "You're the best friend a person could ever ask for."

"You are, too," Gibbs said, a tear rolling down his cheek.

Moss shook his head. "No, I'm about as shitty a friend as exists. I've done nothing but put you in harm's way for years while I sort out my family and every other fucked-up aspect of my life. But I can start to be a good friend now."

"No, Moss, really," Gibbs began but Moss held up a hand.

"Gibbs, I'm done taking from you. I'm done asking for help from people who would rather stay safe while turning a blind eye to people who are angry that they are unable to help. This whole thing is ass backwards and as we head into our final fight, our chance to take down the megas for good and begin to heal this planet, I want to do it right," Moss said. He needed to change things. What came next would require full commitment. "So go be with Ynna. Take care of your wife, take care of yourself. Live a happy life and let me and the Taks of the world give you the one you deserve."

"No, that's not what I was saying," Gibbs sputtered, but Moss continued.

"It was, even if you hadn't realized it yet," Moss said. "Patchwork got shot but will be fine and I can barely live with myself. If anything happens to you… if anything happens to you when you have a kid on the way…" Moss shook his head and grimaced at even the idea of it. "I couldn't live with myself. And not just because Ynna would kill me."

Gibbs chuckled. "She really would…"

"She wouldn't need to, and now she won't have to," Moss said.

"She'll probably bust my balls to smithereens for sitting back when I could be fighting," Gibbs smirked.

"You're right, she probably will, but she will also be thrilled to have you, even if she doesn't say it," Moss told his friend.

"She does," Gibbs admitted quietly. "When it's just us, a lot of that defense mechanism bullshit falls away. She's still tough as nails but without a lot of the bravado."

"And you?"

"Oh, I'm still totally full of shit," Gibbs joked.

Moss smiled. "I wouldn't have it any other way."

"You two will be okay without me?" Gibbs asked sincerely.

"It's not like you're gonna be on the other side of the planet," Moss said. After a while he added, "Yeah, I'll be okay."

"I don't know," Gibbs said with a smile, "you would've died back in Carcer City without me."

"Among many other times," Moss noted, lifting his glass in the direction of his friend. "I wasn't kidding when I said you are the best friend a person could ask for."

"I love you, Moss," Gibbs said raising his glass and taking a gulp.

"I love you, too," Moss told his friend and they embraced. Though he was sad for himself, he couldn't have been happier for his friends. "Carcer City really feels like a million years ago, doesn't it?"

Gibbs laughed and reached behind the counter to fish out another bottle. "It's like another lifetime," he said and the two of them reminisced for a while longer.

Eventually, Moss got a communication from Puck saying, *I found it.*

CHAPTER 12

"The city is reeling from the devastating attack on its water source by ThutoCo. The mayor's office is warning that there are still plenty of polluted sources and advises running your tap for at least five minutes before drinking water," a reporter said on the news.

"The mayor has offered to pay for every citizen's water while this crisis is being sorted out.

"Meanwhile, protesters continue to gather outside of ThutoCo's corporate headquarters in downtown B.A. City. In one poignant moment, a grieving mother laid the body of her deceased toddler at the foot of the stairs of the company. ThutoCo could not be reached for comment, but we are working diligently to hold them accountable for what has happened and will continue to press for answers on behalf of the viewing public."

Neither Moss nor Gibbs were paying attention to the vid screen showing the news as it played for them in the back of the cab. Once he had gotten off the chat with Puck, Moss had let Jo and Tak know that he and Gibbs would be leaving. Jo had given Moss a hug and apologized for clocking him before promising to let them know when Patchwork was okay. Moss had shaken Tak's hand, promising to be in touch about what was next.

Now, in the cab on the way back, they were just quiet. The vehicle banked and began to land, and Gibbs looked in puzzlement out the window as they dropped through the neon-lit fog.

"Chinatown?" he asked.

Moss nodded. "Only be a second. You can wait in the cab."

And it really did take him just a few moments to do his business before they were off again. Within a moment, Gibbs was snoring quietly, and Moss just sat in contemplative silence until they were back in the safe house.

He nudged Gibbs and they disembarked, strolling down the street with their quiet footsteps echoing in their ears.

"How's Patchwork?" everyone wanted to know when Moss and Gibbs reached the bottom of the stairs. Moss updated them as Gibbs put an arm around Ynna and stole her away, undoubtedly telling her of his decision.

"He's doing okay. Jo and Tak are with him, and he is getting the best help dirty money can buy," Moss told them.

Issy wrapped Moss in a hug as Stu, the small circular robot that Patchwork had adopted, looked up at them with its digital eyes and said, "One hundred percent of my owners have been shot. This is a troubling percentage."

"That *is* a troubling percentage," Moss agreed and turned to look at Judy. "Can we talk for a second?"

Issy squeezed Moss's arm and walked away, scooping up Stu and carrying it with her. Judy looked up at Moss with a worried expression and asked, "What's up"

The next afternoon, Moss stood dressed in all black in the Garden of the Sacred Form, a cemetery exclusively for pristiners. Stan had never held the beliefs of his parents, but he had honored their wishes and refused any augmentations to his body. He never took the one allowed by his soccer league nor a replacement arm when we he lost his real one. Despite the other choices he made, he honored his parents in this one way.

Moss had missed the man every single day since he had been killed. He had been the first person to bring Moss into the fold and make him feel at home with this crew. He had introduced Moss to the city, to the sights and sounds and smells, and most importantly to the tastes. Stan had loved food and loved to share his love with others.

A slight breeze blew the grass of the perfectly manicured lawn and Judy squeezed Moss's hand.

"I never thought I'd see this day."

"Puck is a good man," Moss observed. "He spent a long time trying to track this down, and even though he's the head of the company, it took a long time for him to get access to it."

"He's not the only good man," Judy said, turning their wet eyes up at Moss.

He opened his mouth to protest, but the sound of two drudges walking up the hill toward them drew the whole crew's attention. The drudges carried the casket holding the remains of Stanley Wu, saved by the Carcer Corporation for some nefarious reason. Moss guessed it was for personality mapping as ThutoCo had it done to infiltrate them but it was only a guess.

As the robots made their way up the hill, Judy burst into tears and began to wail, pressing themselves into Moss's chest as the others gathered around and rubbed their back and offered words of condolence. They cried as though they were releasing the weight of the world, screaming out the pain and suffering they had been through. It was the sound of their very soul.

The machines continued to the grave and stood on either side, suspending the casket between them. Moss had rejected the cemeteries offer for a pristiner priest, so the two drudges wasted no time and simply began lowering the casket into the rectangular hole lying beside the graves of Stan's parents.

Judy turned their head towards the lowering box and screamed, "Fuck! Stan! I love you! I'm sorry! I need you and miss you!" They sucked in air and blew out snot and continued to sob. They pushed Moss away and ran over to the hole, collapsing alongside it and saying, "I miss you so much. I don't want to go on without you, but I promise I will keep going for you. You were my reason for living but I won't let you be my reason for dying. I will honor you. I will always honor you as you honored me. You are the love of my life and you'll always be the love of my life."

Moss and the others turned away as Judy continued to say all the things they had been unable to tell him. Moss felt tears roll down his own face and he knew he needed this too. Stan had trained him, taught him and made him the man he was today. He had been gone a long time, longer than the time Moss had known him, but he had made more of an impact on Moss than just about anyone in the world.

He turned to look at the hole and remember his friend. He remembered his wisdom, his laugh and his passion. Moss had known so much death, had been the cause of so much death; but this one had been with him for so long and now, letting his friend be buried beside his parents, Moss could make his peace with it.

Judy continued to wail as Charles, Stan's brother, walked slowly up the hill with Stan's great aunt Mei on his arm. Moss had only met Charles recently and hadn't liked him, but he knew it was the right thing to do to invite Stan's family. Moss made his way down the hill and intercepted Mei so Charles could continue up to the grave. The man gave Moss a nod and continued to walk.

"Thank you, young man," Mei said, shooting him a toothy smile. She appeared to be in her eighties but had a youthful aura about her. Having seen her in the kitchen, Moss knew that she still moved pretty well, but she was happy for the assistance after having to walk so great a distance. "Thank you for returning his remains."

Wiping away a tear, Moss said, "I'm just happy we were able to."

"You're a fine young man," she said, reaching up and squeezing his cheek between thumb and forefinger.

"I'm really not," Moss said, "but I'm happy that I can give everybody some closure, and hopefully find some for myself."

"He talked about you as if you are the future of the whole planet," Mei said. "He had been so angry and so frustrated with the people of this world, but you and Burn and Sandra and, of course, Judy, gave him hope. You didn't know him during his darkest days, but I was happy to see that he had found his happiness before the end."

Moss had seen Stan brutalize his enemies but couldn't imagine the man as genuinely dark. Judy had mentioned it and he knew it was a part of his friend's history, but he just couldn't imagine it. "I'm happy he could find that, too."

"I hope you can too," Mei said, and when Moss looked into her eyes, he felt as though she could see his soul.

He looked at Gibbs and Ynna, and then Issy. "I think I will."

"Good boy," Mei said. "Now help an old lady walk up the hill."

"You aren't that old," Moss said with a wink and the woman laughed a deep, throaty laugh.

"You're right," she said as they neared the grave. "It must be all this fresh air and grass. I've lived in the heart of the city my whole life. This might as well be the middle of nowhere."

"Yeah, see, I knew it wasn't an age thing," Moss joked, and she squeezed his hand to let him know that she wanted to join Charles and Judy at the grave. He smiled at her and stepped away so she could shuffle over and join the others.

Moss stepped over to Issy, who looked up at him and smiled weakly. "It's a real shame."

"What part?"

"That he never got to try my dad's cooking," she joked quietly.

Moss cracked a smile. "You're kidding, but he really would have loved it."

"Everyone loves it," she said, turning from the graveyard to look at Moss. In the bright light of day, her eyes glistened at him. "He was written up as one of the ten best East Asian Heritage restaurants in mid-B.A."

He could tell how sincerely happy she was for her father.

"That's great," Moss said. "A bit specific, perhaps, but still great."

"Right, and how many top ten lists have you made?"

Moss draped his arm over her shoulder. "I mean, I was the number one most wanted person in the city for quite some time…"

Issy smirked and shook her head. "Still crazy to think about."

"I know, right? I still feel like a noob who shouldn't be counted as a threat to anyone."

Issy laughed and the sound cut through the air, causing her to quickly cover her mouth. "You may think of yourself that way, but you did just, like, kill a whole bunch of people, like, just yesterday."

"Right," Moss said.

"To say nothing of the… other thing…"

"Sure," Moss said, wishing she hadn't brought it up. "It's possible that I don't see myself for exactly the person I have become."

"Had to become," she corrected, standing up for him when he would not.

Moss shrugged. "I suppose."

Issy laughed again but this time, much more quietly. "Seriously, you are changing the world for the better. We literally just helped keep an entire population from being poisoned to death. There are two sides to all of this. I know the cost has been high for you, and the shadow of all you have had to do will follow you forever, but it's worth it. And more than anything, it's remarkable that you have been able to bear it. Most people could not.

"What you have seen, the situations you've survived, would be enough to psychologically destroy most people, but here you are — on the precipice of something amazing. We may actually be able to turn this ship around before it's too late."

At that, Moss smiled. He looked at the grave and the three people kneeling before it and saying their final goodbyes. "Stan would have loved to know that."

CHAPTER 13

"So, what's next?" Judy asked, wiping a final tear from their face.

Moss smiled. "We go home and figure out how to take down ThutoCo once and for all."

Everyone smiled at that, even Seti, who had joined them a few minutes earlier. Though she acted as their eye in the sky and didn't get into the fights, she had met Stan a few times and had wanted to make her peace too.

"Got any leads for us?" Moss asked.

"Yeah," she said. "Upon Derek Sterling's death, a list was sent to us."

"What kind of list?" Issy asked.

"Pretty sure she's about to tell us," Ynna said, rolling her eyes.

Issy snorted. "I filled a natural break in the conversation. It's called..." she trailed off, looking up and seemingly trying to find just the right words.

"Good one," Ynna laughed. "Real burn."

"In the time you lot did this whole routine, I could have told you," Seti reminded them, letting out a slow sigh but not immediately continuing to speak.

"Well, now you're just fucking with us," Ynna said and Seti laughed.

"Right, I was," she remarked, still chuckling. "He sent us a list of every member, living and dead, of the Amalgamated Interests Council, their supporters and collaborators. We now have the names we need to cripple the entire thing and take them out for good."

"Oh, shit," Moss murmured.

"Yep, oh, shit," Seti confirmed. "I'll ride with you back to your place and we can begin to coordinate our efforts."

Moss nodded. "This is it," he said in shock. "This is actually it."

It didn't feel real. The idea that they could finally cut the head off the AIC and give this planet a chance to move in a new direction was staggering. The future could be bright. The children Moss had met and the ones on the way could inherit a world that wasn't ruled by corrupt greed.

It would take work, lots of work, but it could happen. And Moss knew one thing.

"When we divide this list, I want Arthur Smith."

No one seemed surprised to hear him say that, and they waited for him to continue.

"He is the reason my parents are dead. He is the one who bastardized my father's technology and used it against us. He infiltrated and may have distorted my mind. He is the one who poisoned us, poisoned the city, and I believe he's the one the program in my mind was altered to deal with. He is evil. For me, it couldn't be more personal."

Heads nodded all around and Moss felt Issy's hand on his back. "I'll be right there with you. My father will be happy to know that we are finally avenging your parents." Moss smiled at her. To him, She was the most beautiful person he had ever known.

"We will help Seti get all the teams moving in the right direction," Ynna announced and Gibbs nodded.

"They are going to be a lot of moving parts, so I'll take all the help I can get," Seti said. Her conical cybernetic eyes adjusted and she smiled, brushing graying blond hair behind her ear.

She turned and began walking toward the dropship and everyone fell in behind her. There was a buzz, a certain excited energy among them.

Judy grabbed Moss by his shoulder. "I don't think I can express how much this morning meant to me."

"You don't have to," Moss told them. "I know it already."

"I know that's true, and I know I've already thanked you, but I still just wanted to say it again."

Moss smiled. "I love you, Jude."

"Yeah, yeah, yeah, you, too," they said with an uncharacteristically broad smile and hugged Moss. He had done it as much for himself as for them, but he was pleased that after all the suffering they had been through, they could feel at peace with the partner they loved so deeply.

"All right, that's enough of this sappy, sentimental horseshit, let's get back to killing."

Moss chuckled. "Let's," he said, and they both boarded the dropship.

Everybody strapped in and the ship began to lift off the pad, tilting slightly and moving in the direction of home.

"Anybody else want donut?" Issy asked.

"Ooh, I would eat the shit out of a donut," Ynna said and everyone else enthusiastically agreed. "Oh, chauffeur,"

Ynna called to the drudge pilot, "can we stop at Rolling Pin Donut, please?"

The robot didn't speak, but the dropship change directions and Moss smiled. There had been so much darkness for so long, and despite the fact that they were leaving an impromptu funeral, everyone seemed upbeat. Moss needed this moment and knew the crew did too.

"You know what we should do?" Gibbs began.

"I'm sure you're gonna tell us," Issy said.

Gibbs ignored the comment and said, "We should try donuts from every place we can find in B.A. City."

"I don't know if it's the pregnancy or what, but that's the best idea you've ever had," Ynna said enthusiastically.

"Yep, even I agree with this one," Judy said. "Wait, what the fuck?"

They all felt it. The dropship quickly tilted and began moving toward the ground at a sickening speed. Looking out the front windshield, Moss watched as the ground rushed up to meet them. He heard screams and curses as his body felt a hard impact as the ship slammed into the street and went tumbling head over heels.

Everyone gripped their seatbelts as alarm bells and lights went off. Moss sprayed vomit everywhere as the ship crashed to a halt. Dust and smoke filled the space and Moss felt himself dangling from his strap. The ship had landed on its side, but he didn't think he was too badly injured. Groaning, he snapped the buckle and unstrapped himself with his left hand, gripping a strap with his right so he wouldn't fall on anyone he couldn't see through the smoke. He dangled a moment before easing his feet onto some metal. "Issy!" he shouted as he heard Gibbs calling for Ynna in the choking smoke flashing red in the emergency lights.

"I'm fine, just a little banged up," Issy said from somewhere in the dark. "Go check on Ynna and make sure she's okay."

"I think I am," Ynna called from Moss's left, "but I need to get to a doctor right now."

Gibbs had been sitting beside the door and Moss could hear him working to open it.

"Pretty sure it's pressed up against the ground," Gibbs informed them.

Moss felt a hand on his back and squinted through the debris to see Judy, who made a fist and pointed at their throat to indicate they had been hit in the neck and would have a hard time speaking. Then they gestured with their head towards the emergency hatch at the roof of the dropship. Moss nodded.

"I'm going to open the hatch," he called but felt a tug on his shoulder. Judy shook their head and pointed at themselves before pointing the hatch. Then, they pointed fingers at his eyes before sweeping around the space to indicate that he should help the others. He nodded, knowing that that would be easier for him since he could speak.

"Who's close?" he asked into the dark.

He nearly jumped out of his skin when he felt hot breath right beside his ear saying, "I am."

Ynna laughed, but when Moss caught his breath and turned to look at her, he could see that she was terrified.

"Good one," he said before adding a whisper, "I'm sure the baby's fine."

"Oh, my love," Gibbs said as he appeared through the smoke and scooped Ynna up into his arms. He had some cuts on his face and had clearly been hit with some flying scraps of metal, but Moss was relieved he seemed to be okay.

"We got it," Moss heard Issy call from the hatch, clearly having met up with Judy. Light filled the space though was still impossible to see through the smoke. Gibbs and Ynna moved quickly away from Moss toward the light to get her out of there as quickly as they could.

Moss walked to the front where Seti had been sitting.

"Seti?" he called and heard a sputtering cough in reply. "Shit," he muttered without even having to see her. He moved toward her gurgling sound, waving away smoke to reveal her strapped in a seat near the front. A huge piece of the siding had sliced through her stomach. Her hands grasped vaguely at the wound and she tried to speak but nothing came out.

As he got close, she said, "This is why I never leave my place."

Anger and sorrow welled up within him and he moved close to inspect the wound. He reached to unbuckle what he thought might be the clasp but there was so much blood that it was hard to say what was what. Seti shook her head and Moss watched as one of her eyes telescoped and turned and he immediately felt it.

He saw white for a moment.

"We will have time in here," Seti told him, standing with him in his hex. The cybernetic eyes were gone, and she had what Moss presumed was her face from before. She smiled at him. "Bastard who bought me forced me to get the implants, but I kept them as a reminder of where I had come from."

Moss nodded. "I'm so sorry, Seti."

"It's a pretty shit way to die," Seti said but in a tone that suggested casual complaint more than anger. "Why people in our line of work really shouldn't have kids."

"Or why people with kids should get out of doing this," Moss suggested and Seti smiled, tapping her finger to her nose.

"Should I even ask how you have access to this program?" Moss asked.

"Nah, you already know the answer," Seti said, and Moss nodded. "So," she said, still in that unnaturally casual tone, "I'm going to upload the list to your mind now."

And he saw information begin to fill the computer monitor in the corner of the apartment in the program in his mind.

"We'll see the job done," Moss said his voice breaking along with his heart, "because of you."

"I want a statue," she said in such a deadly serious tone that Moss couldn't tell if she was joking. She seemed to read his expression. "No, really, I want a statue in my honor."

"Seti, I'll name a whole fucking city for you," he said with a smile.

"Thanks," she said quietly. "I believe in you, Moss."

"We're going to be lost without you."

"Yeah, you will be. But you'll figure it out. You always do."

"I don't know," Moss sighed. "Feels like we are up against some pretty insurmountable odds and there are very few of us left."

Seti took a step closer to Moss. "You still have the one thing you need."

"The program?" Moss asked quickly, wanting to know what she knew about it that he didn't. He didn't even care that it was another person who had more information about the thing in his mind than he did; he just wanted to know.

She turned wide eyes on him and said, "Oh, no, I don't want to die."

She disappeared as though someone had pulled the plug on her very existence because, in a way, they had. Moss tried to point back to reality, but as so often happened, he couldn't. He sat on his bed and screamed, enraged with the world and everyone in it.

He felt a hit, hard and painful, and saw the flashing red and the blur coming toward him.

Another hit.

He saw the sunset from the vista where he and Issy had camped. It was pristine and perfect, devoid of the desolation wrought by men.

Another hit and he was back in the dropship, reaching for his gun. He didn't even know what he was firing at, but he kept pulling the trigger until the battery light flashed empty. He heard crackles and explosions and felt heat as seared metal sprayed all around him. He was lying across several seats, and leaning up he saw that Seti was dead, clutching the piece of metal stuck in her abdomen.

Beside her was the drudge pilot who had attacked him and immediately, Moss understood.

CHAPTER 14

"Moss, what's going on, are you okay down there?" he heard Issy call from the hatch.

"No," he cried. "I'm pretty fucking far from okay. Seti's dead."

"Fuck," Issy exclaimed as Moss made his way to the light. "It's pretty grim up here too."

He made his way to the hatch and clambered out, grabbing Issy's hand to pull him the final distance. As his head cleared the metal of the dropship, his mind was filled with the chirps, cries and calls of all of the other teams. Without Seti to filter the communications, all the teams around the city were trying to relay information and ask for help at once.

Mute all, Moss commanded in his mind. He would help the teams once he got a handle on the situation. The street was quiet, but the sounds of distant alarms and screams permeated the air. Most people were likely still in their homes, recovering from the poisoned water, and now there was a new threat.

Gibbs had his rifle up, Ynna was holding her stomach with one hand and brandishing an SMG with the other, Judy was holding up a revolver and Issy a Kingfisher. Everyone was armed and seemed ready, but Moss knew what they needed to do first.

"We have to get Ynna to a human doctor."

"Yes," Gibbs agreed.

"Not my thing, normally, but even I think that's the best plan. What happened down there?"

As Moss opened his mouth to speak, a crashing sound of shattering glass came from the mall across the street from where the ship had been downed. All heads turned and all eyes were trained on the front of the store. Moss knew what was coming as a ragged breath escaped his lips. A car alarm sounded nearby but everybody was waiting. Waiting for the coming storm.

As the glass smashed, the front of the mall collapsed in a shattering wave. Glass blew out of the front as a torrent of drudges streamed toward them. Some were dressed as personal shoppers, others as mannequins and salesclerks. Their metal frames and display screen faces allowed for no confusion about what they were.

Moss and his friends started firing at once and the first row of drudges exploded in a hail of bullets and bolts. But more were coming. Some ran on two legs while others galloped with their arms. To the right, two more crashed out of the bakery, one falling head over heels before standing and charging at them. Moss took two shots, dropping one of the baker bots. Their programming had been so overridden that it seemed killing all humans was more important than their own safety or ability to move.

They kept firing but the drudges were closing in. Judy pulled the massive wrench they carried from their belt and charged towards the drudges, putting their body between the attacking robots and Ynna. They swung and smashed two of the drudges with one motion.

Gibbs continued to pop shots and shifted his body to protect Ynna, moving his large frame to keep himself between her and the onslaught.

Ynna looked equal parts enraged at needing protecting and grateful for the support. As more drudges poured from the store, she fired several bursts into the oncoming crowd. More closed in on Judy and Moss and Issy continued to rain blasts on them. They were closing in and enveloping Judy.

Issy and Moss had the same instinct in the same moment, both hopping down from the side of the ship and racing to help Judy as they continued to smash bots from the middle of a scrum. Without communicating it, they each took a side, Moss breaking left and Issy right.

"Fuckers!" they cried, letting forth another massive swing and sending more drudges flying back, parts scattering everywhere. Issy took one side and Moss the other, taking clean shots to avoid their friend.

Gibbs was reloading as Ynna hunched over, holding her stomach. The sight of it enraged Moss, and as he shot, he let forth a sweeping kick with his cybernetic leg. The force of the machinery was so strong that it swept four drudges off his friend and sent them flying into the air. Three crashed down, smashing against the sidewalk, and one was propelled into the side of the building, hitting it so hard that it splintered some of the bricks.

Two more were rushing Ynna, and Gibbs quickly spun his rifle in his hands and swung it at the approaching robots, cracking one in the faceplate and sending it careening into the other. Ynna didn't miss a beat and wasted the two grounded drudges with a massive blast before wincing again.

"I'm not okay guys," she called out and Moss knew things were bad. He couldn't remember a time when Ynna had ever admitted to being hurt or needing help. Even when she had been shot in the stomach, she had just acted like it was little more than a scratch.

Issy shot down the final two attackers and everyone rushed over to Ynna.

"We have to find me a doctor," she said "We have to be sure the baby's okay."

And that was the priority. Nothing else mattered to any of them except getting Ynna the help she needed.

"Anybody know where a doctor is?" Gibbs asked, worry thickening his voice.

"I don't even know where the fuck we are right now," Judy exclaimed, panting hard from the exertion. They all were gasping for air and drenched in sweat. Looking up, Moss saw that they were on Market Street but didn't have any idea where a doctor was.

Ynna locked eyes with Moss. "Seti's dead?"

He nodded gravely and Ynna's cybernetic eye went black as she undoubtedly searched for a nearby doctor.

Judy asked, "How'd she go?"

"Piece of ship sliced through her," Moss said. "Unceremonious death for one of our fight's greatest heroes."

"And if he survives, her son just lost their mother," Judy observed sadly.

Moss felt as if he had been punched in the face. They had just discussed children in her last moments and she hadn't said anything. Her digital version hadn't said anything. She had used the time to give him information rather than send a message to her child. The thought of it was enough to crush Moss's psyche.

"She was a hero," Moss reiterated. "In the truest sense of that word."

"This way!" Ynna barked, getting their attention as she pointed up the street. "I don't know what we are going to get, but I need to get to somebody."

"Here," Gibbs said, holding out his arms. "I'll carry you."

"Carry my ass," Ynna snarled but Moss could see the hint of gratitude under the bravado.

They hurried up the street, following Ynna as she guided them forward. A drudge crashed out of a fifth story window and smashed into the street, cracking the sidewalk as his metal frame struck the concrete.

"Seems like this protocol was pretty poorly programmed," Judy observed.

"I had the same thought," Moss said. "That may be our one saving grace."

"How many drudges are there in the city?" Issy asked.

"A metric fuck-ton," Judy said.

Gibbs sighed and looked over his shoulder. "Conservative estimates on the forums have it at one drudge for every three people in B.A. City."

"Oh, shit," Issy muttered under her breath. "But you think it's worse?"

"Yeah," Gibbs said. "This is something people have feared as the drudge population increased in the city. Movies have warned us that robotic populations are dangerous and no one seemed to care. Well, a few loud people on the internet cared, but most people were just happy not to have to carry their own groceries…"

"Okay, Gibby, enough with the self-congratulatory preamble," Issy said. "Just tell us how many drudges you think there are in this city."

"I think it's one to one," he said, pointing his rifle up a street.

It was strangely quiet. Downtown didn't normally look like this, but so much had happened recently that it was now the streets were empty. Another crash of glass nearby but this time, a human fell screaming out of a window, undoubtedly thrown by a drudge. The body crunched against the ground with a sickening thud and burst at the front.

It was another grim sight among days of grim sights. They kept pushing forward.

"And that's before what just happened," Gibbs added. "We have no idea how many people died from the water. But it was certainly a lot. To say nothing of the sick. So that, plus being caught completely unawares at an already vulnerable time…"

Moss interrupted, "We get it, things are fucking dark."

"Really dark," he said in response. "Everyone is always so concerned about AI, and they should be; but hackers and trojan horse settings by the manufacturers are just as much of a risk."

"Clearly," Issy said as they walked past the body.

"Around this corner," Ynna said, and though she was acting tough, her terror was showing. Moss watched as she pulled her face into one of determination, but nothing could hide the look in her eyes.

As they rounded the corner, four more drudges looked up from another corpse. No one had to speak. The crew just opened fire and shredded the metal monsters.

"It's like a zombie movie," Gibbs observed. "I mean, not as much the Spore War, obviously, but still."

He was chattering to distract himself from what was happening with Ynna. Moss knew it was his coping mechanism. Wanting to help his friend, Moss said, "Isn't it more like that one with the robots, Term—"

But he was cut off as another swarm came storming out of a restaurant. Black-and-white striped pants rushed at them with glistening knives. A butcher's cleaver hurtled toward Moss and he ducked as he raised his weapon, sensing the moving air of the blade by his head. Opening fire, he dropped the drudge who had attacked him.

The machines were functionally sturdy, but also mass produced as inexpensively as possible in China. They had been designed to break down just often enough to require the purchase of replacement parts and the hiring of a licensed repair person. They could certainly do damage, but they were also easily destroyed as evidenced by the fact that Judy managed to easily smash right through the middle of one without breaking a sweat.

Ynna pointed and Gibbs rushed over and kicked open the door to an apartment complex.

"Badass," Ynna said with a little smile as they all followed Gibbs into the foyer of the building. There was a bank of mailboxes to one side, a wilted potted plant at the other end and an overflowing garbage can. A staircase at the rear of the room led upstairs, the wine-colored carpet at the center worn to little more than frayed edges and exposed splintering wood.

Ynna looked back and said, "Third floor."

They rushed up the stairs until Ynna stopped and clutched her midsection. Gibbs threw an arm over her and helped her to apartment 303 where he immediately began banging on the door. Nothing happened for a long while and then the door behind them opened. They all turned their heads, but Ynna was never one to be caught unawares and fired a rapid burst into the drudge before it even finished swinging the door open.

Gibbs rapped again and screamed, "We need help! We are people and we have an injured pregnant woman."

That was enough and the door swung open. A woman who appeared to be in her early thirties opened the door and waved them inside hurriedly. "Oh my, I know you," she said, looking at Moss.

"Thank you for taking us in," he said.

She ushered them to the right and through a door into a small living room with a medical aid bot and couch.

The young doctor couldn't stop staring at Moss as Ynna lay on the couch, groaning as she writhed. "When I put it out there that I was a doctor willing to help fight the megas, I never thought *you* guys would show up here."

"Well, we are. Can you please take a look at her?" Moss said, trying not to sound irritated because he was grateful for the help.

The woman nodded and rushed into what he assumed was her bedroom to get a medical coat on. She picked up a tablet as she returned to the room and her medical assistant fired to life.

"I guess it's just the drudges who have been programmed to kill us," Judy observed and Moss nodded gratefully.

"If it were all of our electronics, we would already have lost this battle," he noted while the doctor was quietly asking Ynna enough questions to help analyze her.

"If you wouldn't mind leaving the room," the doctor said, waving a dismissive hand in the direction of the kitchen. Moss, Issy and Judy immediately moved into the other room.

"She went from fangirl to doctor mode pretty quick, huh?" Judy asked with a little chuckle.

"I think it was the coat," Moss smirked.

Issy smiled at the joke and changed the subject to the matter at hand, asking, "So, what now?"

"Before she died, Seti gave me the list of all the AIC members and their co-conspirators," Moss said. "I'm going to find a way to override the drudges and reprogram them to hunt down and destroy all of the names on this list, ending the mega's control of this planet once and for all."

Even though it would just be the three of them, Moss smiled with determination as he looked at Issy and Judy. They both opened their mouths to speak at once and Moss felt it. Like a thunderclap in his mind, he felt the punch from the program and saw white.

CHAPTER 15

"**D**ad!" Moss shrieked into his hex. "There are better ways to communicate with me. I'm getting really fucking sick of this."

"I'm sure you are," said a voice Moss recognized immediately. "And I'm really sorry about that. About everything this program has done to you and put you through."

Moss's eyes filled with tears as he turned and saw her face. She looked exactly as she had when he was twelve. It didn't matter that she was little more than a digital construct that his father had mapped. When he wrapped his arms around her, he was hugging his mom.

"What are you doing in here?" Moss asked. "Everyone said you would never."

"I never wanted to," she said, eyes wrinkling with a smile of pure elation as tears of joy poured down her face. "But I'm so happy I did. I'm so happy to see you."

As so often happened in this program, reality fell away and all that mattered was what was right in front of him. In moments like this, he understood the pervasive Mass Illusion addiction. A quiet moment with his long-dead mother was better than most of what the real world had to offer.

"So what *are* you doing in here?" Moss finally asked after a very long hug.

His mother activated the little kitchen countertop, extending stools out of the ground and sitting.

"If I'm here, that means your mind has activated a root protocol and you are finally ready to dismantle ThutoCo."

Moss shook his head. "How… how did you do this?"

"This is my life," she said with a weak smile, but he knew her well enough to know that she was proud of herself. The smile she was trying to mask would sometimes grow into an expression that filled Moss with more pride than any other on the earth. "Your father and I were both at the top of our fields, realizing the company we worked for was going down a dark path. As you know, together we tried to take down the company from the inside and paid the ultimate price. I will never know how the real me felt in those last moments, but I will always know that my last thoughts were of you," she said, unleashing another torrent of emotions.

When they recovered, she continued.

"I never wanted to be in this program or to give you some false version of myself that you could lean on. It always felt wrong and disingenuous and, frankly, harmful. But your father… oh, your father… he was almost too sweet for what we were doing. He wanted you to destroy the company's ability to use his technology for wrong, but your grandmother and I knew that we needed to do more. We understood that there would be backups and that they would continue to do everything that they could to reach their final goal unless they were stopped. If I'm with you now, then we are on the precipice."

"We are," Moss said. He had so many questions, so many things he wanted to understand, but he didn't know the breadth of the program. He understood it was more important to do what needed to be done than to ask personal questions of a program that likely didn't have the answers. "ThutoCo has, presumably with the help of Xuefeng Technologies…"

But his mother cut him off. "Activated the drudges to decimate the human population."

"Yes. If you knew, why not say anything?" It was another instance of Sandra and his parents keeping him in the dark.

She smiled sweetly and extended a hand, running it slowly down the side of his face. "We didn't know. Burn, Sandra and I, when creating this program, tried to outline every possible evil scheme the company was working on. We played the tape forward and tried to come up with failsafes for as many of them as we could."

"Oh," Moss said. "I'm just frustrated. This program, the secrets around it … it's felt more like a curse than a blessing."

For the first time since entering the program, Moss saw genuine heartbreak on his mother's face.

"I'm so sorry, my love, that's not what I wanted from this. When I created it, I added hidden elements to keep you safe. I never wanted to flood your mind with evil schemes, overpowered hacks and mapped personalities. These constructs were designed to be gifts. Like," and a curious little smile crossed her lips, "a little Advent calendar you could use to free the world of some great evil."

"I love the way you think, Mom," he chuckled. "It makes sense why you and Dad were so perfect together, but that's not how it felt. I've just been chasing my tail for years."

"For that, I am truly sorry. I hope you understand."

"I do now. Finally, I understand."

She smiled at him. "I'm so proud of you, Moss. If I am here, it means you have done some truly remarkable things."

Moss felt the pride of being praised by a parent but also the familiar tinge of guilt that he now felt was chained to his legs. "It's come at a tremendous cost."

"All good things do," his mother told him. "I know it's a bullshit platitude but it's also true. Clichés are clichéd for a reason."

"Sure," Moss said. He had heard this before. "But it doesn't make it any easier. I've had to do some things… I don't know…"

She slid off the chair and draped an arm over his shoulder. "It's okay. Having to do bad things for good reasons doesn't make you a bad person."

"Thanks, Mom," Moss said with a weak smile. "I'm not thirteen anymore, though. I don't think in terms of 'good person' anymore. This world is nothing but gray and I know that I operate in some gray space, too. But the memories, the haunting visions of the lives I've ended, they will be with me no matter how much 'good' I do. That's the real reality of being this kind of a person."

"Wow," his mother said under her breath. "I knew you had grown up but hearing that… I see now that you are a changed man."

"I am," Moss said.

"But there's more," she said. He looked up at her, feeling his brows furrow. "Something is in the code. Someone has installed a program that's changing things. My countermeasures are fighting it, but I can see it. It's not just changing the code, it is changing your brain chemistry. This program has become so enmeshed in your mind that they are, for all intents and purposes, one and the same."

"I suspected as much," Moss admitted quietly. "I am myself, but I've also felt another presence. I've made decisions that I don't think I normally would have. It's not just changing and growing but something else. It's like a dark instinct."

"It has to be…"

"Arthur Smith," Moss filled in. "He's probably spent the last decade trying to break down all your work and when he was able to hack my mind, he also left a shit in my cereal bowl."

"Oh, what vivid imagery," his mom said, cracking a little smile. He was surprised she was amused by the comment. His father had tended to treat him like a child, even here; but his mother seemed interested in his changes.

"What were you like?" Moss found himself asking. "I lost you when I was so young. As a child, you're so concerned with yourself and what you need from your parents that you don't try to get to know them as people."

"You know, sadly, there isn't all that much to tell. You made me happy. And your father made me happy. But ultimately, I was a slave to my work. Both the public and clandestine versions. I spent far too little time connecting with you and far too much time retooling the program I would never see used. Now, knowing fully what I am and what I gave up, I would probably do it differently. I'm proud of you and so happy for the good work you will do, but I'd rather be alive."

Moss thought about the words. He wished more than anything that his parents were still alive. He was grateful to have this program, but he wanted to hug them in real life and share experiences with the real people they had been. Despite

147

all that, he said, "You and Dad… you're going to change the world."

"I know, my love," she said thoughtfully, and another tear rolled down her face. Moss wiped it away with a thumb. "Being little more than a program is a pretty miserable afterlife."

"It's more than most people get," Moss observed.

"It's unnatural, is what it is." Her personal philosophy on the matter kept bleeding through and it wasn't a surprise that she had everyone convinced that she would never have put herself in this program. "And it's scary," she said, her eyelashes fluttering with a vague self-loathing, "that I can see the hack in the program. As soon as we finish this, you have to delete it. You have to destroy every last piece of this, cleanse it from your mind."

"I intend to," Moss said. "If I hadn't somehow known that it was going to be necessary for this final battle, I would have already."

"Good," she said. "I'm sure it will be hard to delete the vestiges of me and your father."

"I made my peace with it," Moss told her. "How bad is the hack?"

"My programming is doing a good job keeping it at bay, and it seems like you had somebody in here to bolster it, but the hack is insidious," she said, clearly trying to stay intentionally vague. That worried Moss even more and helped him to understand that he didn't have much time before the hack enveloped his mind entirely.

He wondered how much of what he had done had been influenced by the hack. Was it making decisions for him? Was it influencing decisions he would've made anyway? He would have to sort out those questions in the future, but for now he needed to move forward.

"What should I do?"

When he blinked back into reality, he found himself sitting on the kitchen floor of the doctor's apartment. "The program?" Issy asked worriedly.

Moss nodded. "How long was I out?"

"About five seconds," Judy said, extending a hand. "We were just saying that we were with you till the end and then you began to fall."

"Well, it's the last time," Moss said, taking Judy's hand, but as they pulled him to his feet, they winced and buckled and both fell to the ground.

"Judy?" Moss and Issy said in unison as Judy clutched their side.

"Fuck," they moaned. They lifted their hand from their side; it glistened crimson.

"Doctor!" Moss called to the other room. The young woman was in the kitchen in a second. She took one look at Judy and barked for Moss to help carry his friend into her bedroom. They passed through the room where the bot was checking Ynna's baby.

Judy snorted a laugh and said, "Any excuse to get half naked, huh?"

Ynna looked up, trying to mask her immediate worry for her friend by countering, "Any excuse to stay out of the action, huh?"

They made their way into the doctor's bedroom, which was more cluttered than Moss would've expected, and laid Judy on the bed.

"I have a bag in my closet," the doctor told Moss and he ran to the sliding mirrored door, pulling it aside and finding a leather bag on the ground. He picked it up and rushed it over to her, and she muttered thanks before saying, "Now go back to the kitchen and stay out of my way."

"Is there anything we can do for you?" Issy couldn't help but ask. Moss knew that she didn't like to feel useless and there was so much that needed to be done.

"There is," the doctor said without looking up. "Do as I say and get out of my way."

Issy pulled Moss across the apartment and back into the kitchen, where she hugged him and sighed with exhaustion. Opening the woman's fridge, she found two beers in the door. She handed Moss one and cracked the other.

"And then there were two."

CHAPTER 16

"The baby's fine and your friend is recovering," the doctor said when she walked into the kitchen. Moss and Issy sighed in relief.

"Thank you," they said in unison.

"Smells like a brewery in here," the doctor noted as she pulled bloody gloves off her hands and tossed them in the garbage. "Make yourselves at home."

"We did." Issy giggled like a child. It had only taken a few beers to get them both buzzed, though it was undoubtedly the nervous energy more than the alcohol. They were both exhausted, terrified for their friends and worried for all the people of the city.

They had spent the time drinking, reminiscing and eavesdropping on Gibbs and Ynna as they whispered to one another in the other room.

Moss looked at the doctor again. "We will never be able to thank you enough for everything you've done."

"I'm happy to have helped," she said mildly. "Most people in the city have their own story, their own reason for hating the megas, and are happy you guys are doing what you're doing. It's truly an honor to have served."

Moss's head was swimming. It was another good reminder of why they were doing this. "I must ask one more favor of you," he said. The woman nodded rummaged around in her pants pocket and fished out a digital car key.

"Oh," Moss stuttered, "that's actually not... I mean, we actually do need... but I wasn't gonna ask... well, thank you."

She looked at him in confusion as he took the key. "I was actually going to ask if you wouldn't mind looking after these guys for a while. I think it's safer to lay low here."

She nodded slowly. "That isn't actually optional."

"Okay," Moss said, extending a hand. She shook it and he nodded gratefully.

He and Issy stepped into the next room and Gibbs and Ynna looked up at them.

"We are going to go end this."

"Just the two of you?" Gibbs asked, deep bags heavy under his eyes.

"We will call in reinforcements," Issy said. "But we have what we need," and she pointed to Moss's temple.

"Happy that fucking thing is finally going to be worth it," Ynna said with a characteristic smirk.

"How are you feeling?" Moss asked her.

She leaned up and pointed to the television. "Got a healthy baby and some western Gibbs wants me to watch. What could be better?"

"Liar," Issy said with a snort.

"Ugh, I know!" Ynna exclaimed. "This sucks on ice but..."

"We know," Moss told her. "We know both things."

"Thanks," she said with a miserable smile.

"Feels weird not having you guys for this last big fight," Issy said, looking at the two of them.

"Um, didn't you see that whole hoverbike chase!? That was enough action for one preggo," Ynna said, and Moss couldn't help but laugh in amazement at the memory of her jumping from a crashing bike to the side of a dropship.

"You will forever and always be the most badass human being I have ever met," Moss told her, and he really meant it. Her eyes welled immediately.

"And you have grown into one hell of a person, yourself. For a bub." He laughed and she added, "Anyway, it's kinda fitting that it's you two for the finale. It should be two bubs taking down ThutoCo."

"Should be three," Gibbs said. "Like old times."

Issy laughed. "Dude, you were always the first one to die and we don't have revives in real life!"

Gibbs's face turned red. "I died so you didn't!"

"Yeah, yeah, yeah," Issy mocked and wrapped her arms around him.

When they released each other, Issy leaned in to whisper to Ynna and Gibbs looked at Moss. "I feel like a child hiding out before the last boss fight."

Moss chuckled. "Some mixed metaphors there," he said, "but this is the most mature thing you have done. You always rushed headlong to my side, even when it put you at dire risk. But now, you are staying back to start a family. In its own way, it really is the most grown-up thing you have ever done. Both of you, really."

"For the record, I hate being mature," Ynna said, raising a hand.

Gibbs playfully pushed it down and put a hand on Moss's arm, leading him away.

"I'm sure they can still hear us," Moss said, looking at the girls who were pretending to chat.

"Sure," Gibbs said, shooting them a look, "but this stage direction indicates that we want to have a moment."

Moss smiled as Issy and Ynna began talking in earnest.

"You really think you can do this? You need me to come along?" Gibbs offered, looking worried.

Moss laughed and put his hand on his friend's shoulder, giving it a squeeze. "I literally *just* complimented you on the fact that you didn't make this exact offer."

"I mean," Gibbs said quietly, "we grow and change but fundamentally stay the same."

"I know," Moss said. "I also know that you don't want me to take you up on the offer."

"Yeah," Gibbs agreed.

"I'm so happy for you. You are going to be an amazing parent."

Gibbs blushed. "I'm terrified. I feel like I'm not ready at all."

"I think if you felt ready, it would show that you aren't. And you are a natural protector. You *did* always die so we could finish the level; you kept me and Issy safe so we could win matches. We made fun of you for how you played but never gave you the credit you deserve."

"I knew," Gibbs said. "I blew a bunch of smoke, but I knew."

"Good," Moss said.

"No," Gibbs said.

Moss gave him a puzzled look.

154

"Don't look at me like that. You are coming back from this. The hero survives."

Moss chuckled. "This isn't a movie."

"The hero survives," he said again. "The five of us have to be standing somewhere together and the music swells."

"Okay," Moss agreed. "That's how we do this."

"You know the next play?" Gibbs asked.

"The program gave me one last hint."

"Wow," Gibbs said. "It's never-ending with that program."

"Got that right," Moss agreed. "This time my mom was there."

"Oh, what a mind fu—" he began.

Moss raised an eyebrow. "Close one."

"I know, but it is," he said, chuckling

"You have no idea," Moss told him. "It's a bit much, honestly. I used to love having them to fall back on, even in a digital form. Now that they are knocking me on my ass and lecturing me from beyond the grave, I don't know. I think it's time to move on."

"Trust your instincts," Gibbs said.

"That's just it. It's time for me to be done with all this."

"It's nice to hear that. You have fought so hard to keep it in there."

"The cost to keep it has become too much."

Gibbs's face turned to one of concern. "Yeah, like when you beat that dog abuser to death? Was that the program?"

Moss smiled because his friend understood him so well and still gave him the benefit of the doubt. He believed that Moss would only do something like that under the influence of a corrupting program. Moss, himself, only half-agreed. He knew the desire was there.

In that moment, he wanted to tell Gibbs everything. All the darkness that had pervaded his mind and all he had done. But he didn't want to. Gibbs was still optimistic and Moss didn't want that to change. He didn't need to know everything, there was no reason to tell him.

Moss simply said, "Yes, stuff like that."

"I figured," Gibbs said. "When this is all said and done, we can unpack everything."

"Sure," Moss said, knowing he would never want to tell Gibbs everything and that, after today, nothing would be the same.

"Good. I love you, man."

"You too," Moss said and hugged his friend.

"May the odds be—"

"Don't do that," Moss told him. "You and the doc are the only ones not laid up, so make sure you're keeping everybody safe."

"Even laid up, I'm pretty sure I'm still the one who's keeping everybody safe," Ynna called from the couch. "And yes, we were listening."

"Asshole," Moss said.

"Yeah, love you too," she said and blew a kiss that Gibbs reached out and grabbed before it hit Moss's cheek. He took his balled fist and stuck it down his pants.

"Gross," Issy wailed. "Think of the children!"

Everyone chuckled and Issy hurried across the room and hugged Gibbs. Moss knelt beside the couch and pulled Ynna's natural hand into his own. "You'll take care of him?"

"Moss," she said softly. "I got you. I'll take care of everything. I always do."

Moss smiled at her. "It's really always been you."

"Nah," she smiled. "It's been a team effort. A yin and yang thing."

"I appreciate you saying that," he said, but didn't believe it. In his heart, she had always been more of a leader than he. Both when Sandra was alive, and when she had died, she was the one who had kept it altogether. Moss had been gifted with the program and the lineage, but Ynna worked and fought for her role in the world.

"Now," Ynna said, "go do your thing, I'll see you after."

They high-fived and he headed into the doctor's bedroom where Judy looked up at him groggily. They were propped up on pillows and bandages were wrapped around their stomach, but they smiled weakly.

"Took you long enough," they said with a little smile. "This feels like that movie that Gibbs made us watch with the elves and shit that had, like, fifty-two different endings."

"Ugh, I know," Moss groaned. "And you have to remember that he made me watch it a dozen times before we got to you guys."

"You're a good friend," Judy said in a joking tone but locked eyes with him and added, "I really mean that."

"You've thanked me enough," Moss told them.

Judy shook their head and rolled their sleeves up. "It'll never be enough. When I looked down and saw that I was dying, that I might die just then and there, I realize that I would've been okay with it because I had finally found peace. I was carrying around this weight, this burden, this guilt and anger. I had carried it for so long and now, finally, I've released it."

"Good," Moss said. "I'm happy it helped. And don't forget, thank Puck when you see him next."

"I will," they said and their face softened. "How you doing?"

It took Moss a moment to answer the question because he didn't really know. "I guess I am doing as well as I can be, given everything."

"That's enough," they said. "You ready to kill Arthur Smith? Pretty sure he won't make it easy."

"I know he won't, but I am up for it. Been a long time coming."

"Kinda cool that you can avenge your parents and tell them about it," Judy said.

Moss shook his head. "It's the strangest fucking thing."

Issy walked in and hugged Judy. "You rest up and listen to the doctor, hear me?"

"I hear you," Judy said with a little smile. "Plus, I'm pretty fucked up under here," they said, indicating their dressing. They were looking at Moss and Issy with an unusual serenity that indicated to Moss that heavy drugs were involved. He was happy to know his friend was recovering and feeling no pain.

"Love you, friend," Moss said, moving in after Issy to hug Judy who tried to cover their wince.

"You, too, asshole," they said with a laugh as Moss and Issy moved toward the door. "And hey, don't die."

"You neither."

They walked to the front door and Issy looked up at Moss. "Ready?"

"Yes," Moss said, lacing his fingers through hers. "Let's go save the planet."

CHAPTER 17

Their footsteps echoed off the wall as Issy and Moss made their way into the safehouse. It had been so full of life, but now it was quiet and nearly empty. Stu rolled over with Perro by its side.

Moss knelt and gave both a pat.

"I am not an adequate caregiver for this animal because it requires more than its needs met. It requires love. Love is something I am not programmed to experience, though I sometimes feel like —"

"Yeah," Moss cut off the robot. "Here is the address of where our friends are staying. Go to them but be careful."

"I have seen the news feed," Stu said. "It does not appear that the drudges are any threat to myself or a dog."

"Still," Issy said quietly, kneeling to pet Stu as well, "it's half a war zone out there, so be safe."

"A war zone is not something that can be bisected in the way you described," Stu said.

"You're right," Issy said and booped Stu on the front of its display. "Now, get out of here."

"I will do so," Stu said. Moss and Issy gave the dog one more scratch before he and Stu left the house.

Issy walked over to a couch in the middle of the space that faced toward a firepit with a built-in ventilation system and collapsed.

"I know people are dying, but I just need a second."

"I get it," Moss said as he joined her, flopping down and putting a hand on her thigh. "Better to take a moment now than rush in unrested and getting killed."

"My thoughts exactly," Issy said. "Since I'm trying not to think about the fact that every second we are here —"

"Then don't," Moss said, cutting her off.

She nodded and stared into space, vaguely in the direction of the old underground train's corpse that Tak had converted into a sleeping space.

"It's so much," she said finally. "Seti, Patchwork, Ynna, Judy; it's all just so much."

"You were shot pretty recently yourself," Moss reminded her.

She pointed a finger. "Exactly! It's fucking relentless."

"You remember what you told me the night I learned my parents were killed?"

"No." Issy ran her hand up Moss's arm. "I just remember how you looked. My dad had gotten word from a supervisor that both your parents had been killed in an accident. I was too young to think anything of it but now, looking back, I know that he knew.

"He sat me down and said that you would need me now more than ever. I knew he was right. We were so young, but I understood how you felt, what it was like to lose a parent. I told myself that I would be the friend you needed, that I would be the person you could count on.

"I knew even then, not that I knew that I knew it, that I was in love with you. I wanted to protect you and help you. My dad had always taught me to be tough, but you always seemed so…"

"Weak?" Moss asked.

Issy looked away and grinned. "I mean, yeah, kinda."

"It's nothing I don't already know," Moss said. "For a long time, it was my survival instincts that carried me through this, not my toughness."

"Yeah." Issy started giggling to herself. "I would sometimes get home from school and Dad and I would make fun of how… pathetic… you and Gibbs were."

Moss made a surprised face but he had always kind of known that. "Well, we were lucky to have you then."

"To protect you?" she asked.

"Yes, and because you had the decency to mock us behind our backs rather than to our faces like most people," he said with a little grin.

"Yeah. So, when you showed up that night, I obviously didn't know that ThutoCo had lobotomized your memories or whatever. I just knew you were hurting. You looked so sad, but more than that, you looked lost. You were so distant.

"When you walked in, and you were so pale — I mean, more pale than usual and that hardly seems possible." She mocked him gently with a little laugh. "And my dad brought you to the table and we just ate in silence. It was the longest dinner of my whole life. I just wanted to walk over and hug you, but I couldn't. After dinner, I watched my dad take you to the other room and have a chat with you and I cleaned up the dishes. I wondered what he was saying, wondered if he was saying the same things to you that he had said to me.

"When you walked out of the room, you seemed to be more present. You actually looked at me and saw me."

Moss remembered all of this and wondered if she would be able to remember what came next. It was amazing to think that she already loved him then. Unlike her, he had always known he was in love with her, and he felt like such a fool for all the years they had spent hiding how they felt from one another. He was happy that they finally had shared how they felt, no matter how crazy the road had been to get there.

"My dad pushed you toward me and I brought you to my room. We turned on that stupid show that Gibbs loved and ignored it. I asked how you were feeling, and you said you didn't know. I believed you; I could tell that you didn't know how you felt. You were obviously upset and numb. We were quiet for so long... just staring at each other... and then," half a smile crossed her lips, "you lost your shit. I had never seen anybody cry like that. I must have when I lost my mom, but I didn't have to see it., I had heard of the term 'ugly cry,' but I didn't understand it until that moment."

Moss chuckled. Issy couldn't help being who she was even while recounting. He loved her for that. He loved her for everything that she was, for being there when he was a child, being here now and everything in between. No person had been more present for him in his life. Looking at her now, he realized how truly she was his everything. Now he wanted to just end this fight and be with her.

It was perfect that the two of them would finish it, poetic in its own way.

"You scooched towards me then," he said quietly, "and you put your hand on my back. I knew I was supposed to be thinking about my parents, my sadness, but all I felt was excitement that you were touching me."

Issy laughed. "Boy, seriously… If I had known that, I could've just kissed you and spared us both."

"I wouldn't change it. I wouldn't change anything because all of it brought us here, to this moment, where we can change the world and then be together."

She ran her hand down his cheek and gazed into his eyes. Despite the fact that he had slept with a robot programmed to look like her and shot her unconscious before leaving her, she said, "I wouldn't change anything either."

"You said to me," he told her, returning to that moment in her room all those years ago.

"That no matter what, your parents were always going to be with you…" she recalled, "that, in the end, *you* were the best and truest memory of them."

"Exactly. I thought about that so much. With the program, I have digital replications of them in my mind, but they aren't real. They're code, lines generated by a computer. I am the memory of them. We can delete this program when the fight is over, but I will still be able to honor their memory."

"You've always honored their memory. Even if you didn't have the program, you picked up their mantle and carried it through to the end. They didn't tell you what they wanted from you, what they expected of you, and yet you managed to survive, piece it all together and get to this point. You are them. You will finish what they started."

Moss felt the emotions rise in him as he thought about it. "You are right," he said. Within himself, he could sense them. Not from the program, but through him.

"This reminds me," she said, standing. "I'm going to call my dad. I just want to check in and be sure he's somewhere safe."

"Okay," Moss said. "I'll start getting ready."

He walked over to the footlocker in the train car. Tak had all the seats ripped out and cots installed along one side. The other side had lockers, cabinets and a footlocker that were filled with outfits they might need. Tak had been so proud of himself when he showed it to everyone. He began pulling out different uniforms stolen from many of the major companies. Moss pulled several of them out before finding it.

The feel of the too-often-washed linen was as familiar as his own skin and just holding it made his heart beat faster. There was no reason it should make him nervous, but the ThutoCo engineering employee uniform brought back a lifetime of memories. He didn't know how much of a difference wearing the uniform would make, but if it helped them slip past one guard or one patrol, it would be worth it. He ran his fingers along the fabric, allowing himself to be lost in the memories of an entire life.

Sighing, he began to take off his clothes and get ready for this final chapter. Just before he began to pull the loose, pajama-like pants onto his body, he heard a wolf whistle from the door behind him and turned to see Issy.

"Putting on a show for little old me?"

Moss waved his hand over his thin but fit naked form in the presentational style and smiled. "Like what you see?"

Issy groaned. "The problem is, I actually do."

"Why is that a problem?" he asked, taking a step toward her.

"Because we have more important things to deal with," she reminded him, but she stepped closer to him and now they were within an arm's-length. She looked him over and the moment seemed to overtake her. She pulled off her own shirt and took the last step toward him.

Their lips met and, as it always did, the rest of the world fell away. When he was with Issy like this, nothing else mattered. They had been through so much and they were about to go through so much, it was as if their bodies needed this. All that anger and tension and fear manifested itself as physical desire. The cocktail of other emotions came together in love.

Moss smiled at Issy as he held her on the cot, both of them sweaty and panting but happy. "I love you," he told her, and it was the thing he knew the most in this world.

"I love you, too," she said. She kissed him and jumped up, immediately starting to pull on her BurbSec armor.

He moaned and said, "Wasting no time, eh?"

"Nope," she told him. "*Now*, let's go save the world."

PART III

CHAPTER 18

Looking out the window of the car as it flew over the city was a sight unlike anything either of them had seen. Robotic swarms poured through the streets as people valiantly fought the onslaught. Muzzles flashed under the neon lights, drudges exploded in the diffused light of massive ad holograms and the rain extinguished the fires of smoldering parts.

It was brutal and chaotic, and Moss's heart broke for the people everywhere who were engaged in a war they could never have seen coming. ThutoCo and Arthur Smith had an agenda that had trapped all the citizens of Earth in its web.

Buildings burned and they watched as bodies indistinguishable as man or machine crashed through windows and down onto the street. So much death had been wrought and so much more was planned. Watching part of a global genocide was something Moss thought he would never have seen in his entire life and still couldn't believe. He couldn't understand so great a desire to be rich that a person would be so cruel.

He couldn't believe the people were capable of it and, for a brief flash, he wondered if they weren't worthy of this planet. His sympathy for everyone disappeared as quickly as it appeared and was replaced with a deep disgust. They had coated the planet entirely with glass and concrete, covered up all the wild places and killed all the wild things before turning on themselves. They created robots with artificial human intelligence and then subjugated them as slaves before turning them on each other.

His mind was a soup of emotions, but then he felt a tug on his sleeve and saw that, rather than looking out the window, Issy was looking right at him.

"Think will be a boy or a girl?" she asked, smiling to distract both of them from what was happening outside.

"I don't think it matters," Moss said, shrugging off the question.

She didn't break eye contact with him. She obviously wasn't going to let him disappear back down the rabbit hole she could tell he was going down. Just like that night all those years ago, she knew just how to help him.

"Of course it doesn't matter. It's a totally pointless question."

"I suppose they all are," Moss said, taking a deep breath and trying to be present with her as the car flew over the carnage of the real world.

"All what are?"

"All these questions that we ask ourselves and each other," Moss said. "You know, we talk about these things, but it makes no difference in the world and it's just inane chatter…"

"I think what you're describing is conversation," Issy said with a little laugh.

"Oh, yeah, I think you're right… all conversation is pointless."

"You must be a big hit at parties."

"Ah, yes, I've been told that before," Moss said and winked at Issy. "And you know for a fact that I was never a big hit at parties."

"You were once you talked to people," she corrected. "The problem was that you stood in the corner eating chips and waiting to talk to Gibbs and me."

"What's wrong with wanting to talk to people I know I like?" Moss said and he genuinely wanted to know what she would say.

She rolled her eyes at him. "How do you know who else you might like if you don't talk to more people?"

He opened his mouth to rebut her point but then closed it as he considered what she said. Since leaving the burbs, he had made some of the best friends of his whole life. That kid who stood in the corner eating chips would never have known the camaraderie and love of friends. Issy was right and he had been a fool.

She must have sensed that he was drifting again because she joked, "I'm sure you'd be more than happy to talk at a party if it was all full of bears or tigers or some shit."

He smirked. "I totally would, too. If I can get to know a roomful of animals, that really would be great."

"You really can't hel—" Issy began but the car took a hard turn and began to drop. They turned to look out the window and saw them. Row after row of massive white, beehive-shaped buildings as far as the eye could see. They were bathed in intense lights projected from massive spotlights, giving them a strangely ominous glow in the night sky.

They landed in the plaza outside Burb 2152. Though it was flanked on all sides by different burbs, Moss always thought of this plaza as belonging to their burb. They tucked their weapons away and stepped from the cab. It was eerily quiet here, but Moss knew that most citizens of the burbs had been killed with the water poisoning rather than by the drudges. When they looked inside the surrounding restaurants, they could see bodies slumped this way and that.

Without saying a word, Issy ran over to the restaurant operated by her cousin. Moss walked slowly through the space, listening to his footsteps echo off the building and the quiet burbling of the fountain. He walked towards the restaurant, and it wasn't long before Issy came rushing out with a grimace on her face.

"Fuck these motherfuckers!" she said, spitting as she rushed toward Moss.

He opened his arms in offer of a hug and she blew past them, saying, "No time for feeling sorry for ourselves. Let's go get the chip and end this."

They walked toward the burb.

As the building loomed, Moss's heart rate quickened. It was home. He was back at the place he had spent most of his life. His memories were here. He had lost his parents here. He had met Gibbs here, fallen for Issy here and grown up here. It was so strange being back.

The doors opened before them and they stepped through, setting off the metal detectors. The foyer opened into a wide courtyard with fountains, the animal exhibit, tables and benches, and was surrounded on all sides by shops.

Memories flooded Moss's mind as they stepped into the courtyard and Issy stayed silent as well, undoubtedly feeling the same as he. Then Moss noticed a body just inside one of the shops. After seeing one, he couldn't help but notice all the others. They littered all the shops and lay under the tables. ThutoCo had killed their own people first.

"It's fucking sick," Issy gasped but Moss was distracted, his eyes locked on the small exhibit in the center of the space. There were green trees and grass, a little water feature and a heated rock where the cloned tiger spent most of the time. It was not there. Moss didn't see it anywhere. More than anything else, the fact that so dangerous an animal was gone made him nervous.

"Tiger's not there," he whispered to Issy and watched as the color drained from her face.

"Let's keep going," she said hurriedly.

They kept walking toward the stairwell. He knew the exact one they needed to go to. When Moss had been ten, he had followed his father as he left their hex. At first, Moss had suspected that his father knew he was being followed from the way he constantly glanced over his shoulder. But eventually, Moss realized that his dad didn't know he was being tailed. They had watched the spy movie the night before and Moss thought he was being incredibly cool.

Following as close as he could without being spotted, Moss had ducked behind a potted plant as his father entered the elevators. Moss had worried that he was going to get off on an unknown floor for a meeting, but he had been lucky that his father had simply exited into the main courtyard on the first floor. Moss had held his finger up like a gun as he darted between pillars and tables and decorative low walls.

He had gasped and slammed himself against the floor when his dad looked over his shoulder once before pushing open the door to the nondescript stairwell. Even after all the times Moss had been there, he had never even noticed the door before and waited for just the right time to follow his dad. He exhaled slowly, silently, as he pushed the bar and inched the door open. He saw his father disappear around the corner, descending another level. He wanted to rush but held off, moving slowly and closing the door manually so it didn't bang.

He moved on tiptoes, trying to keep his footfalls from echoing. It was slow going and he felt like he was balancing on the handrail but after a time, he poked his head around the corner to see his dad disappearing into a dark corridor at the landing of the stairwell. The wall snapped shut behind him and Moss took off at a sprint down the remaining stairs, crashing with both palms into the wall and then looking around for cracks or keypad or any indication that this was actually a door. There was nothing.

That night, when his dad got home from work, Moss asked where he had gone. It was the first time he saw his father's face go pale and contort with fear. He knelt, putting his hands on Moss's shoulders and looking him square in the eyes.

"I don't want you to ever talk about this, do you understand?"

At first, Moss thought he was still playing the spy game but when he said, "Moss, I need you to hear me, never speak about this again," Moss knew that he was serious.

"Oh, okay, Dad," Moss said but furrowed his brows. "Why?"

"That's a good question but one I won't answer. You just need to trust me, okay?"

Moss nodded.

Looking back now, the conversation felt so emblematic of his life: the trust he had in his parents, their secrets and the deception of ThutoCo. The moment had felt like nothing at the

176

time, a fleeting conversation forgotten as quickly as it had happened. But now, descending that same staircase all these years later, the moment resonated.

As they reached the landing, Moss reached out with his mind. The construct of his mother had unlocked the program and he had full control over it. He had felt the power once before as he had glided through the air, controlling every drone that came his way. It had made him feel as terrified as it had made him strong at the time, but he needed it now.

He found the locking mechanism with the program and opened the lock, placing his hand on the wall and pushing.

"Neat trick," Issy said.

"Saw my dad use it once. I should have known then."

"Known what? That the company was shady? That your dad worked on secret projects? What?"

As he opened the door, he began to answer but turned as a blur rushed down the white hallway toward him. Moss turned to see the drudge propelling itself toward them, arms outstretched and end affixers open. The metal was closing in on them fast before it stopped completely and fell to the ground.

Neither Moss nor Issy had even the time to reach for their weapons and she looked up at him. "The program?"

He nodded and they both turned to examine the place. Much like the rest of ThutoCo, this secret lab was painted white under fluorescent lights. The long hallway had windows on either side, opening into different workplaces. It seemed to be engineering on the left and more traditional research on the right — lab equipment and other stuff that Moss didn't recognize.

"Know where we are going?" Issy asked as Moss knelt, staring at the machine on the ground. "Moss?" she asked, but he was gone. In his mind, he was pulling at the database, reaching through files to retrieve what he needed.

He could feel the counterbreakers and ThutoCo programs trying to fight him, but he sliced through them like a warm knife through butter. His mother had been too good; Patchwork was too good.

Soon, he saw it, felt it.

He pulled and turned to look down at the drudge he had disabled. The internal machinery whirred back to life and the screen at the front of the humanoid robot booted up. From the little speaker, Moss heard, "Oh, hey, Moss."

"No. Shit," Issy said.

"Hey, MOSS II."

CHAPTER 19

"Did you guys finally get together?" MOSS II asked excitedly. "That's great!"

Moss and Issy both laughed. It was quite an odd thing to be chatting once again with the AI Moss had long considered one of his closest friends. He had known that the program was based on his own personality. But he hadn't known that it was mapped directly, and then learning from the real version in order to eventually replace the real Moss. It was like meeting a version of himself from before everything that had happened, a Moss frozen in time.

"I guess we got out of Africa?" Two said, tilting its robotic head.

Moss laughed. "We did," he said. "Quite a lot has happened."

Two chuckled, the strange, unnatural sound so familiar and yet so distant to Moss's ears. "I expect that is true." The drudge was shaped just like a human and hoisted itself up on its elbows before pushing itself to its feet. "So, what are we working on now?"

"We are going to steal an override program, make you synch with all the drudges on earth, and reprogram them to kill the fucking AIC."

"Use of such language is unadvised and you will be docked one Productivity Point for the day," Two said and there was the hint of a laugh in his tone.

Moss snorted a laugh and Issy said, "I'm pretty sure we are going to end the day with no Productivity Points..."

MOSS II cocked its head and said, "Good. Let's go fuck some shit up..."

Moss and Issy burst out laughing as Two added, "I've always wanted to say that."

They began to stride down the hallway, Moss in the lead, as Two asked, "So how did it happen?"

Issy laughed. "He shot me."

"Fitting," Two said.

Moss looked at them over his shoulder as they continued down the interminable corridor. "That's all you are going to say?" he asked Issy, only half-jokingly.

"Fine," she giggled. "He also fucked a relief aide he customized to look like me."

"You told her!?" Two asked Moss in astonishment and Moss felt himself flush. Even after everything he had been through, the memory of that still embarrassed him.

"Gibbs told her," Moss complained.

"Ah," Two said, his voice from the speaker sounding just like a synthesized Moss. "I should have known."

"Classic, right?" Issy laughed.

"Oh, yes," Two agreed, "should have heard the way he fretted after that one time he said he liked you after you won that tournament."

"I forgot all about that!" Issy exclaimed. "He was so awkward for the next month and I thought it was because he regretted saying it."

"Well, he did, but not for the reasons you thought," Two said.

Listening to the two of them go back and forth was like a strange window into the past. It was as if he was listening to himself and Issy make fun of Gibbs years earlier. He marveled for a moment at his father's technology, and how MOSS II was nearly like a real person. Especially now that Moss deactivated its restraint programming. And even though they were mocking him, he smiled at the moment.

They rounded the corner and Moss saw the door. The room that had been his father's office so many years ago and where he would find what he was looking for. The weapon that could end this reign of terror once and for all. He began running, his cybernetic legs carrying him quickly forward until he felt it.

The punch from inside his brain.

He didn't think there was anything left for his parents to say to him and so as he felt his real-life body falling to the ground, he knew what to expect. As he opened his eyes, he saw the man's face once again.

"Just stop it," Arthur Smith said, looming over Moss. He was dressed in a fine suit and looked like a more handsome version of the real man. He had obviously had his breakers fixing his appearance to match how he thought of himself rather than how he actually appeared. The small, unnecessary vanity did not surprise Moss, who just smiled at the man.

"I'm not going to stop," Moss told him. "You're evil and your company is evil and the company you keep is evil and I'm going to stop you. This unremarkable kid from the burbs is going to take down your entire organization. You've never been able to stop me, and you won't be able to stop me now."

Arthur Smith shook his head. "Of course I'll be able to stop you. Even with all your skills and all your friend's skills, all your family's skills, I was able to get back in here, wasn't I? I got in here the first time and I got back in now."

"You may have gotten in here, but you can't control me and you can't stop me."

"I may not be able to control you, but I will be able to stop you. And, being in here, I can see you. I can see what you've done. You think you're better than me, but you are exactly like me."

Moss felt the rage burning within him. "I'm nothing like you!" he shrieked, though he wanted to believe the words more than he did.

Arthur Smith smirked, and it felt like he could see Moss's mind. "You did what you needed to do and I'm doing what I need to do. You ended a life and I'm ending a life. This planet will be better for it and you know it."

"One. One life," Moss justified but he knew it was more to himself. "You're trying to kill off everyone on this planet."

Arthur Smith's teeth were gritted as he got right in Moss's face.

"You and I both know that humanity is the real poison on this planet. Mother Earth has tried to swat us from her hide since we lit our first fire. Let me help her. Using the wild spaces between the cities, you know that's what this planet should be. If you stop me, humans will leave the city and cover this planet once again in glass and concrete until there's nothing left. We will drive ourselves into extinction and take every living creature on earth with us. You can stop that and all you have to do is walk away."

"All you see is evil in people because you're an evil person," Moss snarled. "But it doesn't have to be that way. I've seen the good, seen the people who are working hard to heal the damage that we do and have done. Once the villains who control the planet are gone, we can put the future of this world into the hands of people who care about it. Research and science can save us from ourselves and heal all the wounds."

Moss watched as Arthur's face contorted before a broad grin crossed his lips and he laughed out loud. It was the condescending laugh of somebody who believed they were listening to a fool.

"You have lived too long and seen too much to believe that," Arthur said in his reverie. "If I have learned anything about you over these past few years, it's that you do see the world for what it is. You are smart. Smart enough to know that I am right."

"I'm smart enough to know that this is a sales pitch that might have worked on other rich assholes but won't work on me."

"It doesn't take being rich to see what we have done to this world," Arthur said quietly. "Humans have a propensity for destruction so deep that we not only massacre every life form in front of us, but also ourselves. We engage in murder, engage in war. Everything human beings set their eyes on ends up destroyed. It isn't just that we suck it dry, it's that we extract everything that we can *and then* burn it to the ground."

He looked Moss right in the eyes. It didn't matter that they were in a program in Moss's mind; it was as real as any conversation he had ever had and Arthur's eye contact was as present.

"You look me in the eyes and you tell me that planet Earth is better off with us than without us."

Moss had to give it to him, Arthur Smith had come up with the perfect argument. He had undoubtedly been studying Moss, trying to get into his head and he had figured out the perfect angle. When all was said and done, the man was a consummate salesman and had found the perfect pitch. But it wasn't going to work.

"Of course the planet would have been better off without us," Moss admitted frankly. "But we are here now, and it can't be undone through murder. What can be undone is the harm we have caused. We humans got ourselves into this mess and we are smart enough to get ourselves out. This planet isn't doomed to be a dystopian wasteland simply because we are on it. It is only this way because of the people we have allowed to rule it. By handing this place over to profit-driven corporations, we have given into our worst nature.

"But it doesn't have to be that way. We can be a planet of hope once again. We can be a people of progress once again. We can save ourselves and all the creatures of this world. You said that we were the same, but we couldn't be more different because, while we both understand the damage that has been done, you see a pessimistic fatalism and I see an optimistic opportunity."

"Then you truly *are* a fool," Arthur said dismissively and shook his head.

"No." Moss heard his mother's voice from over Arthur's shoulder. "He isn't."

"He is a hero," his father said, and Arthur turned just before Moss's parents punched him in perfect unison. The digital Arthur wailed as Moss's parents pounced and beat the program from his mind. With each hit, Arthur crackled and fritzed and began to fade. The two constructs were powerful and proud and fought with the ferocity of parents who needed to protect their child.

With one final blow, Arthur disappeared from the program and Moss's hex was silent. His parents walked over to him, each putting a hand on his cheeks. His eyes flashed back and forth between them as their hands met and they smiled at him. Both had a look of pure pride on their face. He was finishing what they had started, he was honoring their memory and he felt full. His heart swelled and his father smiled at him.

"And I forgive you," he said and it was something Moss had needed to hear since that night on the roof. "I know you just had to do what was right and I'm sorry it was something so hard."

Moss felt a tear burn his cheek as his mother said, "We love you, Moss."

"I love you guys, too," he said through tears of overwhelming emotion.

"We know," his father said quietly.

"Now," his mom said and cracked a smile that he remembered so vividly. "Go save the world."

He gasped and blinked and saw Issy and MOSS II staring down at him. "Arthur Smith knows what we are doing," he warned them. "We have to get moving."

Issy offered him a hand and helped him to his feet.

"I'll admit that I'm not surprised by either what just happened or that revelation," she said and MOSS II shook its head. Her casual comment in a moment like this and little jokes made it possible to keep going. He loved her so much and was happy to keep fighting so that he could share this planet with her.

"And I'll admit that I have a lot of questions about what's going on," Two said.

"So much," Moss said with a chuckle and clapped the robot on the back.

He went to the lab door and opened it, scanning the room with the program and instinctively knowing exactly what to do. The room was not much to look at. There were a whiteboard, a desk, chair and a holoprojector surrounded by cinderblock walls painted white.

Moss plucked a pen from a cup on the desk and walked over to exactly where he knew to go, drawing an X on the wall. He turned to MOSS II and said, "Punch here."

"With pleasure," Two said as it strode over to the spot and punched just hard enough to turn the cinderblock to crumbling rocks.

Moss began to paw at the stones, pulling away chunks until he found what he was looking for. He pulled out the little chip and looked at it. It was exactly like the one Ynna had brought him all those years earlier. It had the personalities and the overrides, and it was one final gift from his parents.

Jamming it in his pocket, he turned and said, "Let's go to The Idyllic Tower."

"That's ThutoCo's headquarters in B.A. City," Two stage whispered to Issy.

"Yes, I know, thank you."

CHAPTER 20

"We must hurry," MOSS II informed them. "Arthur Smith seems to have begun a manual override of my systems."

"Shit," Moss said. "We need you."

"Aww, thanks," Two said. "That means so much to me."

"No, I mean, because... " Moss began.

"Yes, I know," Two cut him off. "You need me to synchronize, I got it."

"Right," Moss chuckled, remembering their easy banter.

"Get a room, you two," Issy joked.

They reached the top of the stairs and rushed into the courtyard. They were purpose-driven and ready to finish what they had started. Issy's hand found Moss's as they rushed toward the front door but the sounds of their footsteps were soon joined by those of others.

"There they are!" Moss heard a voice cry as he saw BurbSec Zetas appear from doorways and up on the balcony that overlooked their position. The Zetas had purple shoulder plates and Moss figured they were Arthur Smith's personal guards. They had eliminated all the rest of the Zetas so Moss thought this was the last remaining unit. They kept coming and Moss began to appreciate how truly surrounded they were as the three crashed into the side of a tall fountain.

They pulled out weapons and Moss wished that he had worn armor instead of a disguise that served no purpose. There was a brief moment of silence before the world erupted all at once. The sound of gunfire and bullets cracking into stone and splashing through water reverberated around the space.

Issy threw MOSS II a gun and the robot caught it with computer precision. "Would you like me to attempt a success calculation?" Two asked.

Moss shook his head and shouted, "Wouldn't be accurate." He turned and easily cut down one Zeta as he stepped out of cover. "We've become pretty good shots."

Issy was paying no attention to the other two and her eyes followed two more Zetas as they tried to flank the three. Moss watched as she fired two shots, piercing the necks of both the attackers.

Having seen both actions, Two said, "I believe our odds have changed."

The drudge tilted its chassis and popped out from behind the wall, firing perfect shots in immediate succession. Drudges were never supposed to be able to kill like that. Their programming prohibited it, but with the restrictions off, Two was able to shoot down enemies with ease. It wasn't the mindless programming of the drudges they had been facing but the perfect melding of computer programming and his own mind's instinct and creative thinking. It was what the program was designed for — melding the best of man and the best of machine. Of course, much like ThutoCo had, this was a misuse of the technology.

Another round of shots rained down on them and Issy shouted, "We're pinned!"

Without having to be told, MOSS II leapt out from behind the fountain, drawing all the attention and fire. It fired as it did, taking down more Zetas. Moss and Issy both popped up and took more shots. By the time the Zetas realized the distraction, it was too late.

Two took one last shot and a Zeta on the balcony cried out before slumping over and falling over the edge, clattering to the ground.

It was silent again. Issy turned to Moss and smiled.

"I assume you have transport?" Two asked hopefully. "The upload is at thirty percent, so we must move."

Issy nodded at Two. "We have a car out front."

"I'll bring it around," Two said hurriedly, obviously worried about how little time they had. It took off at a full sprint, moving far more quickly than any human could.

"Let's end this," Issy said and kissed Moss on the cheek as she wrapped his hand in hers.

They walked toward the door, leaving the burb for what Moss hoped to be the last time.

She squeezed his hand, and he heard the sound in the same moment.

Time slowed to nearly a stop as she pulled down on his arm and he turned. He didn't understand. There was blood. So much blood. On her and on him. Her eyes were locked on his. He blinked at the vision of her face going pale. He didn't understand. It was so pointless. This shouldn't be happening now. She gasped for air, gurgling as he moved to wrap her in his arms.

Over her shoulder, he could see the BurbSec officer clutching his side and brandishing his weapon with his other hand. He was wounded and the gun was swaying as he tried to take aim at Moss. He knew he should fight back, kill the officer before tending to Issy, but he didn't care. Another breath staggered from her lips and a drop of blood rolled out from the corner of her mouth as the officer took aim.

Moss could see the man close one eye and train the pistol right at him. He helped Issy to the ground, exposing his entire head. The officer would have a clean shot, but it didn't matter. Nothing mattered to him in that moment. Everything was pointless. She was dying for nothing. It wasn't poetic or meaningful, it wasn't important or a grand sacrifice to save someone else. It was simple violence at the end of violence.

Issy's eyes drifted upward a moment, losing track of Moss whose wail mixed with the sound of the gunshot. The bullet clipped his shoulder, but he didn't feel it. For just a moment, he glanced up and locked eyes with the man who had killed Issy. This time he had Moss right in the crosshairs.

Moss took a breath, knowing it was his last and not caring.

Then a flash. It was quicker and more graceful than anything Moss had ever seen. The orange coming out of nowhere. It was silent. In all the violence Moss had witnessed, nothing matched this.

The tiger bounded out from wherever it had been stalking them and leapt. It clamped on the officer's neck in a flash of teeth and blood before bringing him down. The animal swung him like a ragdoll, a cat with a bird. The person who had been there a moment before was nothing more than a meal just a moment later. The tiger clamped again to ensure that its prey was dead.

Moss watched in horror and wonder. The tiger turned and looked right at Moss. He felt something, some connection as the animal looked into his eyes and then turned, dragging the body away.

Moss looked down, tears burning his face. Issy rolled her head to look at him. "Moss," she forced, blood pouring from her mouth.

"Don't," he pleaded. "Don't."

Her eyes went vacant again for a moment and he thought he was about to lose her. He let out another wail and her eyes returned to his. "Don't," she said, and he thought she might just be mirroring his words, but she looked at him with determination. "Don't become…" she began but the words died in the air as her eyes went dull.

Moss screamed like he never had. His soul poured from his mouth as he released all the hurt and pain and loss. His throat burned and cried out again. The sound echoed around the burb. He hated the world. Feeling Issy, the love of his life, now just a limp corpse, he didn't want to go on, didn't think he could go on.

A crashing sound came from behind as MOSS II drove the flighted car through the front glass of the building and turned to a stop beside him. It hopped out and stammered, "Oh, oh no, I'm so sorry."

Moss could hear the emotion in the robot's voice., the imprint of himself from the past also losing Issy. But the programming overrode it. "We have to go. Now."

"No!" Moss wailed. "I won't leave her!"

191

"You have to or you lose everyone," Two yelled, stepping over and putting a metal finger on Moss's shoulder.

"No!"   he   shouted. "I don't care about anyone. Fuck them. Fuck them all."

"You don't mean that," the machine pleaded.

"I do! Get the fuck away from me!" Moss yelled, holding Issy tighter. He didn't care about anything. The shock of it all coursed through him.

Two knelt beside Moss and said quietly, "These were Arthur Smith's people. Let's go kill him."

Moss sucked in spit and snot as he growled, "Yes."

Leaving Issy's body was the hardest thing he had ever done. He felt lost and numb and hopeless as Two piloted the car toward the gold-plated building at the far western edge of the city. The monument to corporate greed sat right at the edge of the west, the last building before the ocean. At it came into view, it looked to Moss as a monument to despair.

MOSS II said something he didn't hear. He couldn't hear anything. He was lost. He was alone in the world. He felt as if he had nothing and no one. He was going through the motions now because he wanted to hurt Arthur the way he had been hurt; but the cause, saving the world, helping the people in it, none of that mattered. He couldn't bring himself to care about it. His mind was a dark ocean and even though he was paddling to keep his head above the surface, he could feel the water filling his lungs and his body beginning to give.

"So it comes down to this," Two said as it tilted the car to reveal Arthur Smith standing on the roof of the tower beside a communication array. It was the one Moss's mother had shown him. He knew that he could override the drudges and change the course of human history. Instinctively, his hand went to his pocket, and he felt the chip. All he would need to do was insert it and let MOSS II synchronize with the system. There was only one man standing in his way, the one man that had taken everything from him. The man who had his parents killed and robbed him of Issy.

He was just standing there on the roof waiting for them.

The car lowered and landed. Moss wasted no time, hopping out and pulling his weapon, but as he did, Arthur raised one of his own. Moss wanted to pull the trigger, let them both die and be done with it, but MOSS II cried to Arthur, "Get out of our way!"

Arthur laughed. "You should be happy, drudge. I'm trying to give the planet to you."

Two stepped forward. "I'm not just a drudge, I'm…"

"A real boy?" Arthur Smith sneered. "You're a can opener with cut and paste memories," he said and turned to Moss. "And you… what even are you anymore? Your body is half cybernetic and you don't even know what percentage your mind is yours anymore. You gave your brain over to the company, to your parents, your 'friends' and to me. How much do you even control? The thoughts you're having right now, are they yours? Are they mine? Do you even know?"

The words hit Moss like a bullet. He hadn't known. For so long he had felt his mind slipping. Arthur was right. Or was he? Moss didn't know and he didn't know if *he* didn't know or if the program didn't. He shook his head and blinked, trying to wrap his hands around his own psyche.

He hated Arthur and wanted to kill him but didn't know if it was the hacked program poisoning his brain or his own thoughts. It could be either. His grandmother had been lost to

193

revenge and he was so like her. He had her instincts and perhaps now he was a product of her nature.

"You don't," Arthur laughed. "You don't even know."

"He does," Two justified but Arthur guffawed.

"Need your robot to fight your battles for you?"

Moss shook his head and let the weapon fall from his fingers. He wanted to wrap his fingers around Arthur's neck. He wanted to feel the life drain out of him as he had felt the life drain out of Issy. Arthur Smith dropped his weapon as well and stepped forward.

"I suppose it always had to come down to this," Arthur said, pulling one arm out of the sleeve of his suit jacket, then the other before setting the jacket down on the array. Using what little control over the program he still had, Moss made MOSS II unable to move. He wanted to end this himself.

"It did," Moss agreed and there was a brief pause where nothing happened before Moss rushed toward the man he so hated. Moss threw a wild punch, but Arthur had clearly trained recently and dodged the blow with ease.

Arthur struck Moss hard in the face as he moved wildly and he fell to the ground. His actions were being controlled by anger and they were making him lose control. As he turned to get to his feet, Arthur was already looming over him and he struck Moss hard in the face.

He tasted blood as Arthur said, "Why are you even doing this?"

"For," Moss said, feeling blood trickle from his mouth, but he couldn't find the words. Rather, he couldn't feel the answer. He had been doing it for the people he loved, but right now all he felt was a hole in his heart.

"For what?" Arthur demanded as Moss moved to his feet. "Is there anyone worth saving on this planet?"

Moss tried desperately to connect with the things in his mind that he knew were worth saving: the people that he loved, the children that he had met and the children that were to be. He tried desperately to want to save them but couldn't bring himself to feel it. All he felt was that they were more human mouths, more vehicles of consumption.

"Give this planet back to Mother Nature," Arthur said, and Moss remembered the eyes of the tiger, remembered the baby bears in the woods and the woods themselves. For a moment he went to that place but then he saw Arthur Smith's grinning face and knew that the corrupted program was winning.

"No," Moss said, regaining his mind and rushing towards Arthur. The older man went for a punch but Moss deflected it with a forearm and swung with his right hand, breaking the man's nose. Arthur cried out and clenched his nose as blood began to stream down his face.

Arthur kicked as hard as he could, but Moss saw the blow coming and deflected it, the man's foot finding nothing but metallic leg. Moss grabbed him by the collar and punched him in the eye. Arthur scratched and flailed against Moss's face, spitting blood at him, but Moss had the upper hand. All he had needed to do was return to himself. He was a far more skilled fighter than Arthur Smith and had a much higher tolerance for pain.

He hardly felt anything as he hit Arthur again and again. For his parents. For Sandra. For Issy. He beat him for all of them until Arthur's face was a mess of gore. Skin flapped and blood poured as Arthur lifted his hands in utter defeat and Moss

195

dropped his collar. Arthur fell back, gasping for air, but Moss could hear the rasp and knew his lungs were filling with blood.

He let MOSS II go from his hold and the drudge said, "We have less than a minute."

Moss began moving toward the array, fishing the chip from his pocket. He was miserable and exhausted, but he was going to end this.

He felt himself spinning and saw Arthur. The man had a weak hand on Moss's shoulder with just enough force to face him toward the city. "Look at this," he wheezed. "Look at this city."

Moss saw the sea of cement and glass, of steel and neon lights. He saw the high-rises, the streams of flying traffic and the belching pillars of acrid smoke. He saw the cesspit that was B.A. City. As he collapsed to the ground, Arthur turned Moss back to the sea. The sun was rising behind him; the ocean glowed gold. Pelicans skimmed the surface, gliding gracefully.

It was beautiful and serene.

"Let my program upload," Smith said from the ground. "Don't let us be the extinction event."

His eyes followed the birds and then turned back to the city. There was nothing natural. It was all man-made. Arthur was right. If he gave the planet back to the humans, they would simply destroy it.

He pulled the chip from his pocket and dropped it to the ground. He was tired. There was nothing to fight for. He would let the program run its course and let the people die. The planet would go back to nature. The reign of man would end.

As he lifted his foot to destroy the chip, he saw Arthur smile before dropping his head. His body went limp.

Moss had avenged them all.

He had done it.

He was happy for that at least, but his mind was gone.

As Arthur died, it felt as if Moss's mind burned. The rage surged within him and he brought his foot down.

But it didn't make contact.

He felt his body crash backward.

He was hunched over, pressed against a power box.

He didn't understand.

Looking down, he saw blood.

He had heard a shot but hadn't felt anything.

His ThutoCo linens were slowly turning red. His hands were pressed against his belly. Arthur Smith had died; there was no way he could be the attacker. In utter confusion, Moss looked up and saw MOSS II picking up the chip.

Moss smiled as his vision began to blur.

The AI had done what needed to be done. Two had seen the corruption of the program on Moss's mind and had shot him to save the planet. The version of himself from before all this still had that instinct. The same instinct that had saved Moss time and again would now save the world. MOSS II had done to Moss what he had done to his grandmother.

Moss laughed as Two inserted the chip into the array.

The drudge turned as the lights began to flash green. He strode over to Moss.

"I'm sorry," it said.

Moss shook his head. "Don't be."

"You understand?" Two asked.

Moss nodded. "I understand." He could feel the life seeping from him. "If it hadn't been a mortal wound, I could have used the program to stop you."

"Precisely," Two said.

They did share a mind though their roads had diverged.

It was over. It was all over now. The drudges would stop hurting the innocent and would now go after the AIC. The corporate rule of earth was over. Ynna, Gibbs, Judy and all the others would help heal the world.

"Can you help me with something?" Moss asked and Two didn't need to be told what.

He wrapped a metal arm around Moss and lifted him to his feet, carrying him a short distance to lean him to face the sea. Light crept over the ocean as the sun rose. He thought he saw the spout of a whale and smiled. The sound of lapping waves grew louder, the smell of ocean air permeated his nose, and MOSS II draped an arm over his shoulder as Moss closed his eyes for the last time.

THE END

NOTE TO THE READER

Thanks for reading *Drudge Match: A Cyberpunk Saga (Book 7)*!

If you made it to this point, I will never be able to express my gratitude to you. *Into Neon* was the fulfillment of a lifelong dream to share my stories with the world and the fact that you have followed Moss's journey through to the end is so inspiring to me. So, from the bottom of my heart, thank you!

I normally beg for reviews here, and if you want to do it then I will be eternally grateful, but this time I should mention something different. If you want more from this world or want to be the first to know what I am doing next, consider joining my mailing list. I tend to only send one correspondence a month so you won't be spammed but you will be alerted as soon as there is a new book, preorder or other fun news. Thanks again

https://www.thutoworld.com/join

AUTHOR BIO

Matthew A. Goodwin has been writing about spaceships, dragons and adventures since he was a child. After creating his first fantasy world at twelve years old, he never stopped writing. Storytelling happened only in the background for over a decade as he spent his days caring for wildlife as a zookeeper, but when his son was born, he decided to pursue his lifelong dream of becoming an author.

Having always loved sweeping space operas and gritty cyberpunk stories that asked questions about man's relationship to technology, he penned the international bestselling series, A Cyberpunk Saga. His passion for the genre also inspired him to create and cofound Cyberpunk Day ™, a celebration of all things high tech / low life.

He is now expanding his science fiction universe into space.

GLOSSARY

- **AIC (Amalgamated Interests Council)**: An illuminati of business owners working together to control planet earth for profit.
- **Atheletiskyn**: A Dermidos (under D) brand suit to be worn during exercise to monitor all vital signs.
- **Audon**: German luxury car manufacturer.
- **B.A. City**: Northern California megacity.
- **The Betweens**: A colloquialism for the space between the cities.
- **Bovidae Biotechnics**: South African cattle producer.
- **Breaker**: Hacker
- **Bub**: Slur for someone who grew up in a burb.
- **Burb**: Corporate apartment structures where employees can work from home and have all their needs met.
- **BurbSec**: Burb security.
- **BurbSec Zetas**: ThutoCo's corporate military.
- **Carcer Corporation**: Private military force used by many cities as a police force.
- **Carcer City**: A prison city run by the Carcer Corporation. There are several such cities.
- **CerebralSync**: Brainwave controlled digital experiences.
- **Comph**: The largest clothing brand in the world.
- **Conka**: Popular slot machine style gambling device.
- **Crassun Emergency Services**: For-hire fire and emergency medical treatment with additional at cost transportation to your nearest hospital. They also do corpse removal.
- **Cybermesh**: Digital fabric.
- **D2E**: Internet provider and entertainment company.

- **Dermidos**: An electronic full-body suit with many features from cloaking to temperature control depending on the model.
- **DigPlate**: Optical enhancement device that replaces an eye with a computer.
- **DLI**: ThutoCo company currency.
- **Dronepack**: A dangerous and illegal form of personal transportation- a metal backpack that can move operators via flight.
- **Drudge**: A robot with vaguely human shape manufactured and sold by Xuefeng Technologies.
- **Dyeus Industries**: Company that established the first off-world colonies.
- **Esodo Automotive**: Italian flighted car manufacturer.
- **Fibermail**: A strong, bullet resistant mesh worn under armor plating.
- **Foddier**: Food synthesizer.
- **Graymaker**: Electronics dampening device.
- **Great Black**: Outer space.
- **The Great Pandemic**: A period of disease that killed much of the human population and forced people into walled-off megacities.
- **Gro4All**: Vat meat producer
- **HackAd**: Digital advertisement that utilizes neural implant to advertise directly to the brain.
- **Hex**: Individual apartment within a burb housing unit.
- **HoloAds**: Holographic advertisements.
- **Holoprojector**: Machine that projects holograms.
- **Hoplite Motorcycle Club (MC)**: A worldwide 'one-percenter' gang whose members typically ride motorcycles.

- **Kingfisher Munitions**: Electronic weapon manufacturer.
- **Legion Motorcycle Club (MC)**: A worldwide 'one-percenter' gang whose members typically ride motorcycles.
- **Lenscreen**: Digital contact lens.
- **Levitengine**: Thruster on flighted vehicle.
- **The Mass Illusion**: The most popular virtual reality
- **Miners Football Club (FC)**: The premier soccer team of B.A. City.
- **Neo Dark Age**: A time of economic and government collapse that followed the Great Pandemic.
- **NeoVerge Industries**: Company formed by off-world rebels after breaking with Dyeus.
- **The Night Crystal**: Carcer Corporation headquarters in B.A. City.
- **Opperistic Wealth Network**: The largest international bank.
- **Palmscreen**: A touchscreen-based smart devise cybernetically sewn to a user's palm.
- **Pristiners**: A sect of people who believe the human body should not be augmented.
- **Prophet Root ("P-Root")**: Genetically engineered plant whose root can be processed into food, stalked and leaves into materials and helps to restore the environment.
- **Quix Fix**: Chain of 24-hour urgent care facilities
- **REGNAD display**: In-helmet digital display for security officials.
- **Relief Aide**: Humanoid robots (manufactured by Atsuko AndroiTech) used for pleasure by humans.

- **RENTec Building Associates**: Large building ownership group.
- **RePurp Industries**: Salvage company that uses pieces scrounged from the world outside the major cities.
- **Rises**: B.A. City neighborhood where all the businesses were built out on platforms that jut out from the sides of former apartments.
- **Scuba**: Nomadic raiders who live outside the city walls. So named for the breathing apparatus they wear.
- **SeaDome**: ThutoCo vacation complex.
- **Smartshades**: Sunglasses with cellular and mobile computing functions.
- **Suggi-O's**: A synthetic, sugar-based meal in a can for children.
- **Teotl Coffee:** An American multinational chain of coffeehouses and roastery reserves headquartered in B.A. City
- **Thermaskyn**: A Dermidos (under D) brand suit to be worn during exercise to monitor all vital signs.
- **ThutoCo Bioengineering**: Company that provides electricity and genetically modified crops.
- **Tomar LTD**: Mexican food manufacturer.
- **Vat Food**: Laboratory grown food products.
- **Wall Burg**: B.A. City neighborhood which abuts the wall around the city.
- **Warden**: Carcer Corp senior officer. Permitted to collect Carcer bounties.
- **Xuefeng Technologies**: Chinese drudge manufacturer.

Made in the USA
Las Vegas, NV
26 December 2022

64193756R00127